CYNTHIA HICKEY

Cowboy Hazard

Cynthia Hickey

The Cowboys of Misty Hollow

Copyright © **2024 Cynthia Hickey**
Published by: Winged Publications

This book is a work of fiction. Names, characters, places, and incidents are the product of the author's imagination and are used fictitiously. Any resemblance to actual events, locales, or persons, living or dead, is coincidental.

No part of this book may be copied or distributed without the author's consent.

All rights reserved.

ISBN-13: 978-1-962168-72-4

To all my readers who eagerly await the next book. I appreciate you!

Chapter One

Blair Oakley listened as her boss, Jason Duvall, reported a missing teen girl in the nearby town of Misty Hollow. In her mind, she already packed the things she would need. Most importantly, her search and rescue dog, Diamond.

"Blair, once you check into the local motel," Jason said, "head out to the Rocking W Ranch and meet up with a..." he rifled through papers on the table in front of him. "Maverick Browning. He helps with search and rescue in the town and Dylan Wyatt, the ranch owner, said he would be more than happy to show you around. I don't have to tell you that time is of the essence. There's a crowd gathering in two hours to start the search."

No, he didn't have to tell her to hurry. The first forty-eight hours were the most vital for a missing person.

She grabbed the file he handed her. She'd never been to Misty Hollow, but while her boss talked, she'd looked up a map of the area on her laptop. A heavily wooded area. The missing girl...she glanced at the file...Brittney Pitts, could be anywhere.

"The girl's parents said she never got on the bus for school. Fifteen-years-old, blond, blue-eyed, straight A student. Doesn't appear to be a runaway, but don't count that out. Leave immediately and keep me posted." Jason nodded and left her office.

With the file the only thing she needed from her office, Blair headed to her apartment to pack and pick up Diamond. Her dog greeted her at the door, tail wagging.

"We've got a job to do, girl." She let the dog out into the small yard that came with her bottom floor apartment before heading to her bedroom. She tossed a week's worth of clothes and her revolver into a small suitcase. The file she laid on top before zipping the suitcase closed and sending her neighbor a text that she would be gone for a few days.

Within half an hour, she'd loaded the SUV and hit the road, Diamond sitting in the front passenger seat, her head hanging out the window and tongue lolling. Blair laughed and patted the dog's head.

The town of Langley where she lived was only half an hour drive from Misty Hollow. She'd have plenty of time to check into the motel before following her GPS to the Rocking W Ranch.

The motel looked as if it sported a new coat of salmon-colored paint. She could smell the fresh fumes when she exited her SUV and marched into the manager's office which smelled stronger. The walls sported a white so bright she squinted.

"Need a room?" A young man smacked his gum.

That was why she was there. "Yes. I'm not sure for how long. I'm here to search for the missing girl. I trust my dog is welcome?"

"Since it's a working dog, yes, but you'll have to pay a deposit. Refundable if the animal doesn't tear up the place." He took her credit card, swiped it, then handed her a key.

"She won't." Blair smiled and returned to her vehicle.

After stowing her bag in her room, she punched in the address to the ranch into her GPS and headed up the mountain. Truly a beautiful place adorned with the bright green of spring. Since she was early, she took her time to enjoy the drive before turning onto the ranch.

A sprawling three-story house came into view. Several vehicles were parked out front where a crowd gathered near a porch. Standing off to the side was a group of men in cowboy hats. Saddled horses waited near a paddock.

"Let's go to work, girl." Blair shoved open her door. Diamond bounded out after her.

Her boots crunched gravel as she approached the house. One of the cowboys strolled to greet her.

"Miss Oakley?" He thrust out a hand. "I'm Dylan Wyatt, owner of this ranch. We are very glad you're here." His gaze fell on Diamond. "And your dog."

"Thank you. Tell me what you know."

He reiterated what Mark had said and added, "Let me introduce you to Sheriff Westbrook. He knows more than I do." He waved over another man in a cowboy hat. "Sheriff, this is Blair Oakley, Search and Rescue."

Another handshake. "We're glad you're here. Everyone I've spoken to said this isn't like Brittney. That she would never take off without letting someone know where she was going. Her friends never saw her that morning. She never showed up at the bus stop." He lifted a tee-shirt from the porch railing. "She wore this the day before she disappeared."

"Thank you." Blair took the item of clothing. "Why are we meeting here and not at the bus stop?"

"The bus stop is right outside the gate of this ranch. Brittney lived half a mile up the road."

"Then that's where me and Diamond will start."

"Let me introduce you to your partner. We'll all pairing up. Maverick!" He waved over a large man with hair the color of coffee.

When he joined them, eyes the color of a summer sky landed on her. She could see burn scars through the scruff he wore on his face.

Her gaze flicked to his hands. More scars. This man had been through tragedy and walked away, but not unscathed. "It's nice to meet you, Maverick. Care to join me on the road?"

He gave a silent nod and fell into step beside her.

Okay, the strong silent type. She didn't mind the absence of conversation while she worked. She didn't want the distraction, although the man's woodsy aftershave might be more of a distraction than she wanted.

~

Maverick thought he detected a trace of Native American in the woman's inky black hair and slightly brown skin, although the steel-gray eyes kept her from looking completely Native American. He followed her to the road where she held the sweater up to her dog's nose.

"Find her, Diamond."

The dog sniffed, then headed to the left away from where the girl lived. Behind them, the sheriff called out for folks to mount up or start walking, spreading out to form a long line.

The dog let out one bark and took off like a bullet.

"She's got a trail." Blair sprinted after her.

Not to be left behind, Maverick did the same. Soon, they'd left the rest of the group behind. The dog changed direction and headed into the thick woods. Not long after, she set up a frenzied barking.

"She's found something." Blair increased her speed.

Maverick caught up to them. Tangled in the limbs of a low-hanging oak tree was one of those things females used to tie their hair into a ponytail. A few blond strands blew in the breeze. No other sign of the girl.

The dog whined and walked in a circle.

The trail disappeared.

"How can someone disappear in thin air?" Blair frowned.

"Maybe she was carried from here."

As if just realizing he stood there, she jerked her attention to him. "I suppose. Drat."

"Here are some tracks." He pointed out a man's size eleven. "Looks fresh." He followed them, leaving her to join him or not.

"Diamond, come." Blair caught up and fell into step beside him. "You any good at tracking?"

"Fair to middling." Better, in fact, but Maverick wasn't one to boast.

"Ex law enforcement or something else."

"Something else. Military PD." He stifled a sigh.

Conversation was not his thing.

"Nice. Diamond, search." She motioned the dog's attention to the tracks when they started to disappear.

The voices calling out for Brittney cut through the trees and startled birds into flight. A squirrel scolded overhead.

Usually, Maverick enjoyed a walk through the woods, but doing so because of a lost child gave the experience a whole new meaning. A bad one. Seeing the tracks led him to believe the girl hadn't left on her own. She'd been abducted, and they might all be too late to save her.

After an hour of walking, the dog stopped at the edge of a dirt road. Footprints switched to tire tracks.

Someone had taken Brittney Pitts away in a vehicle.

Maverick turned as the sheriff joined them. "She's gone."

The sheriff's face darkened. "I'll call in the FBI. This missing person case has turned into a kidnapping. Unless, she went with a friend, which I doubt since her footprints disappeared only to be replaced by a man's." He turned his attention on Maverick. "I'd like to deputize you and have you work this case with Miss Pitts. Any objection?"

A ton. "No, sir."

Just like that, Maverick was thrust back onto the battlefield where he'd been searching for a lost little boy. He'd found the child in a burning shack. They'd both barely got out alive.

Maverick still carried the scars. This wasn't the same. He wasn't being asked to dash into a burning building.

Chapter Two

Blair sat inside a diner named Lucy's and perused the menu. Enough of a variation to satisfy any palate and all good Southern home-cooking. The top of the menu stated the chef was a four star.

Really? Then what was he doing in Misty Hollow, Arkansas and not Los Angeles or New York?

"You here to find Brittney?" A woman with bright red hair that could only come from a bottle stood at her table, notepad in hand.

"I'm here to try." Blair smiled and handed over the menu. "I'll take the ham and cheese omelet, hash browns, and wheat toast."

"That your dog out front?" She jerked her head toward the window.

"Yes, ma'am. She's a search and rescue."

"We'll send her some eggs and bacon if that's all right with you. Her food is on the house. I'm Lucy."

"That's kind of you. Thank you."

"No problem. We like dogs here, especially working ones. I'll have your breakfast right up."

"Is it okay if I question some of the diners about Brittney?"

Lucy frowned. "You can try. Most folks around here are pretty closed-lipped until they get to know you." She headed for the swinging doors that blocked the kitchen from the rest of the diner.

Blair turned in her chair to survey the other diners. A few cast curious glances her way, then ducked their heads when they caught her looking. Surely, they'd be willing to answer her questions to help one of their own.

Taking note of an elderly man in overalls at the counter, she got up and strolled his way, pasting a smile on her face. "Good morning. I'm Blair Oakley, Search and Rescue. Did you know Brittney Pitts?"

"Sure did. Her family owns the bank here." His gaze looked from her eyes to her feet and back and again. "Search and Rescue, huh? I heard tell that someone carried her out of those woods and drove off with her. I'm guessing her parents will get a ransom note soon enough."

"Why would you say that?"

"Her folks got money. Why else take her?"

There were a lot of reasons young girls went missing. Blair could be wrong, but she didn't think there would be a ransom note. "What can you tell me about her?"

"The girl? Not much. Didn't cause trouble. Mr. Pitts is sitting over there. Why not ask him?"

She glanced over to where a man sat reading the morning newspaper. "Thank you. I will." Noting her breakfast had arrived, she returned to her table to eat and continue studying the other diners. Especially the father.

When she finished eating, she paid her bill,

checked on Diamond who licked an empty plate, then slid into the booth across from Mr. Pitts and introduced herself.

"I've already spoken to the sheriff." He folded his newspaper and laid it next to a half-empty cup of coffee. "My heart can't take much more drumming things up. My baby girl is missing. My only daughter. The wife and son are devastated."

Interesting that he didn't add himself to that list. "This won't take long. The more I know about Brittney, the better chance I have of finding her."

He crossed his arms and sat against the booth back. "You and that dog able to follow vehicles?"

"It's quite possible we'll pick up the trail again." She folded her hands on the table. "We won't stop looking as long as there is a glimmer of hope."

"It's been a little over twenty-four hours, miss. My glimmer is fading."

She narrowed her eyes. Most missing people weren't even searched for until twenty-four hours had passed. "Can you give me a list of her friends?"

He frowned. "You're acting like law enforcement."

"I used to be a police officer, Mr. Pitts. Old habits are hard to drop." She pulled up a note app on her phone.

He rattled off a few names, all girls. "If she had a boyfriend, I didn't know about him." He removed his wallet from his pants pocket and handed her a school photograph. "This year's photo. Take it. Wife has more at the house."

"Thank you." Pretty girl with a sweet smile. If her photo was to be judged, Brittney didn't look like the type to run off.

After a futile attempt to question a few of the other diners, she decided heading to the local high school might be a better use of her time. After she got permission from the sheriff. She'd learned early in her career not to step on anyone's toes.

As she headed outside to unhook Diamond's leash from a light pole, the sheriff pulled up. "Just the man I wanted to see."

"Miss Oakley." He tipped his hat and smiled.

"I'd like to question some of Brittney Pitts's friends. Would that be alright with you?"

He nodded. "You do whatever you feel necessary to find this girl. The FBI should arrive this afternoon, but we can still use all the help we can get." His smile faded. "If you feel anything is off, don't enter into a dangerous situation. Contact my office."

"Thank you." She motioned for Diamond to come and opened the passenger side door to her SUV.

The principal at the local school, a newly built red-brick building, greeted her and introduced himself as Mr. White. "You can use the conference room. Just tell the gals in the front which student to send for. We'll accommodate you in any way." He patted Diamond's head. "Bringing the dog will help the students feel calmer. I'll be in my office if you need me."

The first student to enter the room, a cute brunette, hovered in the doorway. "Am I in trouble?"

"Not at all." Blair gave what she hoped was a reassuring smile. "I'm Blair Oakley. This is Diamond. Please have a seat." She waved to the chair across the table. "I only want to ask a few questions about Brittney."

"Amber Miller. My grandfather owns the mercantile." The girl's face fell, and tears shimmered in her blue eyes. "I can't believe she's missing."

"The two of you are friends?" She thought it best to keep things in the present. They had no need to believe Brittney was dead. Not yet anyway. She set a notepad on the table in front of her for notes.

"Yes. Besties. We always shared a seat on the bus." The girl fell into the chair.

Diamond laid her head on the girl's leg.

"She didn't show up at the bus stop?"

"No, and Brittney was a real stickler for being on time." She shrugged. "She was kind of anal about time. A real A-type personality."

"Had she ever missed the bus before?"

"No. She prided herself on perfect attendance. She came to school even if she was sick."

"When was the last time you spoke to her?"

"On the phone the night before. We always talked about what went on at school that day." She absently patted Diamond.

"Any trouble at school? Anyone she didn't get along with?"

"Everyone liked Brittney. She was head cheerleader, real popular, and belonged to the Beta club. She worked part time after school at the coffee shop."

Blair made a note to question the coffee shop owner. "Boyfriend?"

"No, not that the boys didn't try, but she wanted to focus on her grades so she could get a scholarship. Her parents could afford the college tuition, but she wanted to do things on her own."

"Any boy that seemed overly persistent to get her attention?"

"Maybe Vince Matterson. He's new but shot right to star quarterback. He thought that since he was such a bigshot, he should have the prettiest girl in school." Amber tilted her head. "You're pretty. I bet you were popular in high school."

Blair laughed. "Nope. A total nerd."

"Do you think Brittney is still alive?"

"I'd like to think so. Unless we learn otherwise, I'll continue to believe she is."

When the girl had nothing more to add, the next student, an African American named Deshanay Roberts entered and sat in the seat Amber had vacated. She cast Diamond a wary glance.

"Don't worry. She doesn't bite." Blair turned her notepad to a fresh sheet of paper and repeated the same questions to Deshanay, receiving almost the same answers.

Same with the next two girls, Rosie Perez, Hispanic, and Amy Shuford, Caucasian. The last student Blair had called in was the quarterback.

"I didn't spend much time with Brittney." The handsome boy topped six-feet sat and crossed muscled arms.

"I heard you were fairly new to the school. How do you like Misty Hollow?"

"There isn't much to do outside of sports, outdoor activities, and the movies. You a cop? I ain't seen you around here before."

"Search and rescue. I'm here to assist the sheriff in locating Brittney." She gave a smile that had started to feel forced after an hour of questioning. "Heard you liked Brittney."

He shrugged. "Everyone did."

"Heard you wanted to date her."

"All the football players did."

Blair leaned forward. "Why are you referring in past tense?"

"She's gone, isn't she?"

"Doesn't mean she's dead."

"Don't most missing persons get found dead?"

"No." Blair sat quietly for a few minutes. Something about the boy felt…false. Almost as if he was hiding something. "Do you have an after-school job?"

"Football doesn't leave much time for that. I mow lawns in the summer. Sometimes bale hay. It helps me keep in shape."

"Any idea what happened to Brittney?"

"Someone took her."

"Any idea who?"

"Transient?"

"What makes you say that?" Blair quirked a brow.

"Lots of things have happened in this town, or so I've heard. Bad things. Looks to me like one of those happened to Brittney. She was such a loner outside of her cheerleading friends that I don't see her running off. Know what I mean?"

"Sure do." She noted down a note to check further into the boy's background.

"What are you writing?"

"Just taking notes so I don't forget anything."

"If you don't have any more questions, I need to get back to class. The teacher is going over stuff for a test. I've got to keep my grades up and without Brittney to tutor me after school, I'm in trouble."

Why had no one mentioned the fact that Brittney tutored before now? "Who else did she tutor?"

He rattled off two more names of football players. "She didn't make a lot at the coffee shop and was saving for college."

"An all-around good girl."

"Yeah, I guess, but a bit of a tease, you know. Smiling at everyone, being nice to everyone…yeah. All the boys wanted a taste of Brittney Pitts." He stood, towering over Blair.

Diamond bristled.

"A taste? What does that mean?"

He grinned like a shark. "We all wanted more than she was willing to give."

Chapter Three

Blair's interviews at the school had left an uneasy feeling in her gut. Especially the one with Vince.

Once suspecting foul play as in kidnapping by a stranger passing through town, she now wondered whether something else was at work. Could the boys Brittney had rejected have something to do with her disappearance? Another student altogether?

She stopped at the principal's office and knocked, entering when he called her in.

"How did the interviews go?" He closed a ledger on his desk.

"Puzzling. Do you mind?" She glanced at the empty chair across from him.

Surprise and curiosity flickered across his face. "No, please. What can I help you with?"

"I've been told that Brittney was very popular here at the school."

"That's true."

"Yet, I detected a thread of animosity, especially with Vince Matterson." She put a hand on Diamond's head to make the dog sit.

"I'm not aware of that." His brow furrowed. "But the boy is used to getting what he wants. Still, I doubt he'd harm her."

"What about the other cheerleaders?"

"Absolutely not. That group is inseparable."

She sat silent for a moment. "No fights between them ever?"

"Not that I'm aware of." He folded his hands on his desk blotter. "You can't seriously believe one of the students is responsible for Brittney's disappearance."

"It would explain why she went with them so readily. From what I've been told about her, I doubt she'd have gone with a stranger." The girl seemed too smart. "Even children are capable of violence, Mr. White. Given the right circumstances."

He shook his head. "We've never had anything like this happen at our school."

"How long have you been the principal?"

"A few weeks." He sighed. "I'm usually at the elementary school, but the high school principal retired. I'm going back and forth."

"So, you don't really know the high school students very well."

"No, I guess not." He sat back, rigid in his chair. "It's awfully early to jump to such a conclusion, isn't it, Miss Oakley?"

"Just a gut feeling." She'd learned a long time ago to trust her instincts.

He glanced at the clock on the wall behind her. "Today is early release day. School will be letting out in a few minutes, and I need to be outside."

Taking that as her dismissal, she stood. "Thank you for your time."

She led Diamond back to her vehicle and waited as students swarmed from the school after the bell rang. Spotting Vince getting into a beat-up older model truck, she turned the key in the SUV's ignition and followed him. She wasn't ready to give up on the notion that the boy might have something to do with Brittney's disappearance.

He turned right out of the school parking lot, drove through town, and exited onto the highway. She lost him when he crossed the railroad tracks seconds before the barrier went down to allow a train to speed past.

She continued up a small winding hill. A glance in her rearview mirror showed the young man now followed her. Coincidence? She didn't think so, especially when she increased her speed, and he did too.

She drove until coming back around to the tracks, crossed, and pulled into the sheriff's office parking lot. Vince sped past honking his horn as if he were a friend saying 'see ya'.

Should she let the sheriff know of her suspicions? No, she needed to either find more proof or discount the boy.

Instead, she backed out and parked in front of the coffee shop. Now was as good a time as any to question Brittney's employer.

The shop was full of high school students. Amy Shuford gave a wane smile from behind the counter when Blair entered. "What can I get you?"

She ordered a blended mocha drink and a cup of whipped cream for Diamond. "I'd like to speak to Brittney's boss, please."

"Mary! This lady wants to talk to you." She called out to a middle-aged woman filling a display case with sandwiches.

"Be right there." The woman wiped her hands on her apron. "What can I do for you?"

Blair introduced herself. "Is there somewhere we can talk in private?"

She eyed Diamond. "We don't usually allow dogs in here."

"She's a working dog."

She pursed her lips. "Fine. We can talk in my office." She led the way down a short hall, past the restrooms, and ushered Blair into an office a little bigger than most walk-in closets. She took a seat behind a small metal desk. "This about Brittney?"

"Yes, ma'am. What can you tell me about her? When was the last time you saw her?"

"She worked the day before she disappeared. Brittney was a nice girl, a hard worker. Tutored football players on the day she didn't work here. Amazing how she kept her grades up despite being so busy." She sniffed. "A real tragedy, her disappearing."

"What do you think happened?"

Surprise shined in her eyes. "What do I think? Well, I have no idea. I can tell you she wouldn't have gone off without telling her parents. Like I said, she was a good girl. No drugs or running around with boys. She had big plans for her future and wouldn't let anything come between her and those plans. Someone took her." She swiped a hand over her eyes. "Check the mountain, Miss Oakley. Lots of things go on up there."

Blair widened her eyes. "What sort of things?"

"Dark things. The last few years have seen a lot of

trouble in our town."

"Any newcomers?"

"Only you."

Blair thanked the woman for her time and left. Outside, she sat in her vehicle and thought about the conversation. Misty Mountain rose in the distance. If Brittney was up there, how long could someone last? It wasn't winter, so a person would have that going for them.

It was time to ask for some help. She headed for the Rocking W Ranch.

A woman who identified herself as Mrs. White answered the door at Blair's knock. "Come on in. Maverick is out but should return soon. Stay for supper. We've plenty for you and that gorgeous pup."

Blair opened her mouth to object, then caught the delicious aroma of something bubbling on the stove. "I'd love to."

~

Maverick hesitated in the doorway to the dining room at the sight of Blair laughing and filling a bowl with beef stew. The other cowboys seemed enamored and showed off, cutting jokes. Maverick took his job as foreman seriously, and the last thing he needed was for his men to be distracted by a pretty face.

Still, they were off the clock now, and he couldn't dictate what they did with their free time. "Miss Oakley."

"Maverick and please call me Blair. Do you have a minute after you eat?"

So, she was here on business. "Sure." He sat across from her as Dylan and his family joined them all at the table.

Maverick grabbed two biscuits from the basket being passed around, then handed the basket to Blair. "Best get one while there are some to get."

"Thank you." She took one biscuit and set it on top of her stew. Once it soaked up the juices, she used her spoon to push it to the bottom. "I love beef stew."

"This is venison, dear." Mrs. White patted her shoulder.

Blair's smile faded.

"You don't like venison?" Maverick arched a brow.

"I've gone all these years without trying it, I'm happy to say."

"Think of it as a very lean beef." He grinned, then squelched the grin as fast as it appeared.

"What brings you to the ranch, Blair?" Dylan asked.

"I'm here to ask Maverick to lend his tracking skills. Someone mentioned Brittney might be somewhere on the mountain."

"Lost?" His wife, Dani, asked.

Blair shrugged. "I don't know if she would be lost or held somewhere. Between Diamond and Maverick, I'm hoping we can pick up a trail starting with the dirt road the tracks stopped at."

"It'll be getting dark soon." Maverick frowned.

"You've never tracked in the dark?" She tilted her head. "It lends a new perspective you don't get in the daylight."

"Of course, I've tracked in the dark." Did she think him incompetent?

"Great. Will you help me?"

"The sheriff did ask me to."

She frowned, then shrugged and took a bite of her stew.

He didn't know why he acted so surly. The woman seemed nice enough. Competent at her job, he supposed. And the good thing about tracking at night meant he wouldn't be pulled away from his work during the day. Not that he would complain. Not with a missing girl out there, but he didn't hold out much hope of finding her.

"How long have you been in search and rescue?" Dani handed one of her twins a napkin.

"Five years."

"Always find the person?"

"Yes." Her face fell.

"Alive?"

"No. Not always." Blair took another bite of her stew. "This is good."

"Everything Mrs. White serves is good." Maverick got a second helping.

"You're sweet." The cook patted his cheek. "Even when you're acting like a brute." She laughed. "Our Maverick is always serious, but he's a good man."

Blair's bright gaze landed on him. "I can see that."

His face warmed and he bent over his meal. How could she tell anything about him in the short time since they'd met? When he'd finished his second bowl, he stood. "Can you ride a horse?"

"Sure can." She stood and carried both her bowl and his to the kitchen sink.

"Meet me at the barn." He marched from the room and outside.

A few minutes later, her dog at her side, she

entered the barn. "Hard to track on horseback, isn't it?"

"It's only until we get to the road. It'll save us an hour." He tightened the cinch on one of the mares, then tossed her the reins. "Meet Daisy. She's mild enough and will follow my horse, Trigger."

"I know how to ride, Maverick." She led the horse outside and swung into the saddle as if she'd been doing so her entire life. "Follow, Diamond." The missing girl's sweater hung from her saddle horn.

Maverick nodded and climbed onto his horse's saddle. "There's a flashlight in the saddlebag behind your saddle, along with a bottle of water. We might be gone a while."

"I've got no one waiting for me to return to the motel." She clicked her tongue and set Daisy moving.

They rode in silence as the sun started to set, something it did early on the mountain. A slight breeze blew away the heat of the day and eased some of the stress from Maverick's shoulders. Riding had to be his favorite thing in the world. Something he did when life's memories plagued him. He appreciated the fact that Blair didn't feel the need to make conversation. Instead, she seemed to study the trail they traveled.

He moved ahead of her as they neared the road. Since the road bordered the Wyatt land, few vehicles traveled it outside of hunting season. Across the road lay government land. A place crawling with hunters during deer season. They should be safe enough from being accidentally shot this time of year.

He swung from his saddle, Blair did the same, and looped Trigger's reins to a low-hanging branch. "They'll still be here when we get back unless they're spooked by a coyote."

Her eyes widened in the moonlight. "Are their many around?"

"A few. Keep your dog close." He pulled his flashlight and water bottle from his saddlebag. "They won't bother humans, but they will attack a dog."

"Stay close, Diamond." She retrieved the sweater, her backpack and other things, then held the sweater to the dog's nose. "She won't find anything unless they left the vehicle, if they left in one, but if they did resume their hike, she'll find the trail. You're here as her backup." She grinned.

He'd been many things, but backup to a dog wasn't one of them. "Let's go find the girl."

Chapter Four

Blair stood to the side as Diamond and Maverick searched for a clue as to which direction the vehicle allegedly carrying Brittney went. Times like this she felt helpless. She knew a little tracking but didn't have the nose her dog had or the skills she'd been told Maverick did.

Heavy clouds scudded across the moon and cast the area into an almost complete darkness. Far off thunder promised rain. Things were about to get a lot more difficult.

"I don't see where the truck turned around here." Maverick waved her over. "So, at this point, we follow the road and try to see whether they left the vehicle at some point."

If they did, Diamond would pick up the trail. Flashlights aimed in front of him, they hiked down the middle of the weed-grown dirt road. Thunder rumbled closer and the wind picked up, whipping her hair from its ponytail. No matter. She'd searched for missing persons in every type of weather. At least it wasn't bitterly cold.

Diamond ran from one side of the road to the

other, nose to the ground. She'd stopped every few minutes, glance at Blair and whine, then resume her search. She wouldn't stop searching until Blair gave her the signal.

She glanced at Maverick. The scruff on his face visible when the moon peeked through the ever-increasing cloud cover. Strong and silent, handsome, she couldn't quite figure him out, only that the scars beneath the scruff showed him to be a survivor of something tragic.

She squelched the desire to ask him questions. The man didn't seem to like conversation much. Neither did she while working, usually, but he was an enigma.

"Tired?" Maverick's words cut through her thoughts.

"No."

"Tireless, huh?"

"A young girl is depending on us. I don't quit." She never had before and didn't intend to start now. "You?"

"No, ma'am. I can go all night."

Blair didn't know when she'd call off the search for the night, but it wouldn't be for a while. At least not until the clouds released their burden and made the search almost impossible.

Diamond barked ahead of them, spurring Blair into a run. "She's found a trail."

Maverick studied the ground where the dog had first barked. "Tire tracks, then one set of footprints again. Male. Same ones we found at the start."

"She's still being carried?"

"Yes, if we're following the right trail and not off

on a wild goose chase."

"We have to follow every lead." Time could be running out for Brittney Pitts. She stopped and listened. "Did you hear that?"

"What?"

"It sounded like an engine." What if they weren't alone out there anymore? When the sound didn't come again, they continued to follow Diamond, letting her occasional bark lead them in the right direction.

A light rain started to fall. Soon, the tracks could be wiped out completely. A few minutes later, the rain plastered her hair to her neck.

"Can the dog track in the rain?"

She nodded. "For a while anyway." But not for long. Even Diamond's nose couldn't track through a steady downpour.

The thick trees lessened the rain falling on them, but even they wouldn't hold up under an onslaught. Water started to drip from the branches.

A twig snapped to Blair's right, freezing her in her tracks. She peered through the night, ears straining to hear another sound. An animal finding a place to shelter the storm. She increased her pace and caught up with Maverick.

If he didn't seem concerned, then she shouldn't either. The forest carried many sounds. It was the darkness that made her jumpy. That and the thought that Brittney had been taken against her will.

What if they and the rest of the town was wrong? Even good girls could change and do something unexpected. Blair was a prime example. A nerd in high school, she'd snuck out one night and gone on a joy ride with a boy she'd had a crush on. A ride that had her fighting him off at the end and resulting in rumors the next day that she might be shy but get her alone and she was a tiger.

Was that why she distrusted Vince? Because she'd had to protect herself from a boy just like him? Maybe, but she hoped she could be impartial and not compare him to the boy from a long time ago.

The sound of something scuffling through the brush didn't stop her this time. She continued putting one foot in front of the other as Maverick did. She'd take her cue from him as to when to worry. The man knew these woods far better than she did.

They came upon Diamond on the bank of a creek. The dog ran back and forth, nose to the ground. Blair's heart fell. The dog had lost the trail.

By now, the rain fell in a steady torrent.

"We need to take shelter and continue the search when the rain lets up. This way." Maverick turned off the trail, leaving her to follow.

"Come, Diamond." Blair called out and plodded through the rain.

With a whine, her dog followed, shoving her snout into Blair's hand.

"I know. We'll try again later."

She struggled to keep up with Maverick's long-legged stride but refused to ask him to slow down. The man obviously knew where they could take shelter from a downpour so thick she could hardly see his back through the drops.

They stepped into a clearing. Standing at the edge of the tree line was a tiny building on stilts with decaying wooden steps. "Is that safe?"

"It's all we've got. This deer stand hasn't been

used in years, from what I've been told. Let me test it before you come up."

Maverick put his weight on one step at a time. The staircase shook a bit but held. He opened the weathered door. Vacant other than spiders spinning webs in the corners. "Come on up."

Rain dripped through a hole in the roof, but most of the place looked dry enough. He parted tattered curtains and perched on one of two three-legged stools.

Blair entered and glanced around. "Lovely."

"It's dry for the most part." He turned off his flashlight then wrapped his arms around his midsection. "But not exactly warm."

"Thank goodness it's summer." She sat on the other stool. Diamond plopped to the floor, causing a cloud of dust to ascend. "Are there many of these stands around?"

"A few. Most deer stands are just perches on a tree." He stifled a groan. She would want to talk while they waited for the rain to ease. A fate worse than death. She'd ask about his past, his hopes for the future. He didn't think ahead farther than the next day, content to remain foreman at the Rocking W Ranch for an indefinite amount of time. Hoping to stave off the coming conversation, he leaned against the wall and closed his eyes.

"Aren't you too chilled to sleep?"

"No. I can sleep anywhere under any circumstance." Most of the time.

"Hmmm." The floor creaked.

He cracked one eye open to spot her standing in front of a window shining her flashlight outside. "You might want to save the batteries."

"Right." She turned it off. "The rain is really coming down."

"Uh huh."

"How do you like working at the ranch?"

He sighed and opened his eyes. "I wouldn't be there if I didn't like it."

"Am I bothering you? Conversation is a great way to pass the time." She pulled her stool closer to the window and continued to peer out.

"What are you looking for?"

"Anything and nothing." She folded her arms on the windowsill and rested her chin on them. "How long do you think we'll be up here?"

"An hour or so."

"Ugh. I hate idle time."

So did he, but he didn't feel the need to fill it with talk.

"What do you like about your job?"

"The horses." They didn't talk too much.

"Yeah, animals are great. Diamond is my best friend. She goes everywhere with me, even to bed."

"I don't like dogs in the bed."

"Well, that's your prerogative, I guess."

He could barely make out her form in the dark, but thought she grinned.

"Oh, no. The horses are left out in the rain."

"They'll be fine." He shook his head and closed his eyes again.

"I don't encourage conversation when I'm working, but you really don't like talking at any time, do you?"

"Not unless I got something to say."

"Fine. We'll sit here in silence, so the time drags."

Fine with him.

Not even five minutes passed before she started talking again. "How well do you know this mountain?"

"Well enough."

"Are there a lot of places to hide a person…living or dead?"

"Yep. Lots of hunting cabins up here. A cave or two."

"We should probably check them all out."

"Yep. Will take time."

"You seem rather lackadaisical about this missing girl."

He opened one eye. "That's what you think? What's the point in getting worked up when we aren't sure whether she's even in danger?"

"Because she's missing?"

He leaned forward, his feet hitting the floor with a thud. "Until we know she didn't take off after a fight with her parents, I don't see the need to suspect the worst."

"My gut says something is wrong, and my gut is rarely wrong."

"We are assuming she's in danger. Otherwise, I wouldn't be out here on a night like tonight."

"Next time, we should go during the day."

And there would be a next time, of that he was certain. He figured Blair wouldn't stop searching until she found something. Neither would he, but he wasn't going to jump to worst case scenario unless he had reason to.

He resumed his dozing position against the wall while she prattled on about a high school boy who rubbed her the wrong way. Boys would be boys. Football players tended to have big egos. Didn't mean they'd harmed the girl. Still, Maverick would keep his eyes and ears open around town. If the boy needed watching, someone would say something to that effect. There weren't many secrets in Misty Hollow that stayed hidden for long.

"Of course, I'm not wrong about searching at night giving a different perspective. The weather didn't cooperate." She started pacing, rubbing her hands up and down her arms. "I can't believe how chilly it is this time of the year."

"It's raining."

"I know that! Mrs. White was right. You are surly."

"I believe her exact word was brute."

"Add insufferable, rude…"

"Boorish, boring, stick in the mud…"

"Yes, all of those."

A smile stretched his lips despite him not wanting to participate in conversation. "Loner is another word to describe me."

"Uncommunicative." She moved back to the window. "How long until the men you work for decide to come looking for us?"

"Why would they?"

"Because we've been gone a long time, Maverick."

"Daylight, I reckon. That's hours away."

"I'm going to die of boredom."

"Try catching some sleep. It's about ten o'clock."

"I'm not sleepy."

"Suit yourself." He actually wished he could see

her face. Normally pretty, he bet she was beautiful when riled. Those amazing slate-gray eyes would sparkle. High spots of color would pinken round cheeks.

He gave himself a mental shake. He'd vowed a long time ago not to enter into a relationship. Not after his almost fiancé had run off with another man over five years ago. All because of the personality traits Blair had listed off. Well, Maverick wouldn't change for anyone. What you saw was what you got.

"There's someone out there with a flashlight. No, wait. There are three."

Chapter Five

Diamond growled, her hackles bristling.

Maverick joined Blair at the window. "Strange there would be folks out in this kind of weather."

"Do you think they're searching for Brittney?"

"I doubt it. Come on. We need to check it out. There's been poaching going on and since I've been deputized..."

She really didn't relish going out in the rain. But Maverick helped her with her job so it was only fair she return the favor. Hopefully, those out there were nothing more than teens with too much time on their hands.

"Stay behind me."

"Diamond will alert us to any danger. Besides, I'm armed." She patted her backpack before slinging it over her shoulders.

"Doesn't do much good zipped up." His mouth twitched. "Please tell me you know how to use a gun. I've seen too many folks carrying one who had no clue how to use one."

"Ex-police, remember?" She rolled her eyes and pulled her weapon from the pack, tucking it into her waistband. "Let's go get wet."

"You can stay here where it's dry."

She shuddered. "No, thanks." Even if those in the woods weren't a danger, she didn't relish staying in an unfamiliar place, in the dark, alone. She had Diamond, but she'd want to send her with Maverick as backup. There were things in the dark no one should have to face alone.

"What's wrong?" Maverick frowned, his gaze sharp.

"I'm not a fan of the dark. I got lost once...as a child. Took three days to be found." She patted her dog's head. "It was a dog just like Diamond that found me."

"Hence the reason you're doing search and rescue."

"One of them, yes."

He nodded and opened the door to the deer stand. "I still want you to stay behind me. I don't trust folks who venture out this late in the rain."

Neither did she. She squared her shoulders and followed him into the downpour. Within seconds, rain dripped from her hair and soaked her clothing. It would be a miserable night. "By my side, Diamond." She patted her leg.

The dog glanced up and fell into step beside her.

Maverick trudged toward where they'd seen the lights.

The shadows seemed to come alive around them. The rain petered out. Every rustle and snap of twigs sent shivers down Blair's spine. Evil lurked in the woods so palatable she tasted it. The moon flirted with the clouds, adding to the ominous atmosphere.

Diamond's growls echoed, warning them of the unseen threat.

Maverick glanced over his shoulder. "Okay?"

"Yes." She nodded and shoved her hair away from her face, straining to see the lights again. Anything to cut through the inky blackness surrounding them.

She clutched her backpack, her heart pounding and kept her gaze locked on Maverick's strong back.

"Maybe we should've called for backup."

"Without proof a danger exists? We continue. I need to report back as to who is out here."

The lump in her throat refused to dissipate. Doubt crept deeper into her mind like tendrils of mist. What if they were in over their heads? What if what they found was far more sinister than either of them could imagine? What if they were lost!

Sweat beaded on her brow despite the coolness of the night. She wanted to ask him if he knew where they were going but didn't want to show the fear threatening to freeze her steps into place.

A twig snapped nearby, eliciting another growl from Diamond. Maverick reached for his flashlight, his movements slow and deliberate, while Blair withdrew her weapon. A moment later, his flashlight beam pierced the darkness, illuminating the gnarled roots and twisted branches that snaked across the forest floor.

"Watch your step." He turned the beam to low.

Something moved in the underbrush. A fleeting shadow that sent her heart into her throat. Her pulse went into overdrive as adrenaline coursed through her veins, and she tightened her grip on her gun.

"Someone is out there." Her voice rose barely

above a whisper.

"We did see the lights." He shot her another glance. "Come on. Let's check it out."

Absolutely not. She followed him into the brush, wanting to be anywhere but there. What if they found Brittney? Maybe the lights they saw *were* searchers who had located the missing girl? She held onto the hope that things would turn out okay.

The ground started to slope, and Blair sent Diamond ahead of them. With the dog leading the way, they descended into a valley. The three lights they'd seen flickered on. The forest seemed to close around them. Branches tangled in Blair's hair like skeletal fingers. She stopped to untangle herself.

Maverick's light faded as he moved farther away from her.

"Wait." She forced the word from her tortured throat. Tears stung her eyes. She yanked herself free, losing some hair in the process. Her scalp burned. She rushed forward, tripping over an exposed root and fell flat out on the damp forest floor.

"You okay?" Maverick rushed back to help her.

"You were leaving me." She gripped his hand.

"Never." He pulled her into a hug. "It's okay, Blair. Me and Diamond are here. We won't let you get lost."

"Are we lost?" Her question sounded muffled against his chest.

"No, ma'am." His chest rumbled.

"Are you laughing at me?" She pulled back.

"Of course not." He cupped her cheek. "Rest assured that I know this mountain. There's a cabin not too far from here. I'm guessing those with the lights are headed that way. Unless I'm wrong, it's going to pour again in a few minutes."

"We'd better hurry then." She hefted her pack more firmly on her shoulders.

The cabin soon loomed before them. Dilapidated, looking as if a strong wind would blow it down. No lights flickered in the glassless windows. A fireplace rose on one side promising warmth if someone had left behind firewood.

~

Maverick raised a hand, hesitating for a moment before pushing the door open with a creak of rusty hinges. The only light came from the flashlight clutched in his hand.

It didn't look as if anyone had been there in a very long time. Dust covered the floor. A few planks lay scattered about. He frowned. They look as if someone had purposely placed them close enough together to walk on.

"Can we start a fire?" Blair asked softly behind him.

"I don't see why not." He shined his light toward the fireplace. A few logs sat haphazardly on the hearth. He bent and peered up the chimney. His light went all the way through. At least the chimney wasn't blocked or home to some rodent. "I'll have a fire going in just a minute."

He reached on the mantel and pulled down a rusty tin can which, thankfully, held a few matches. Soon, he had the beginnings of a fire. "Pull up one of those stools. You'll be warm soon. I want to take a look around outside before I join you."

"Take Diamond." Her voice shook.

"I'll be right back, Blair. I promise. Keep the dog with you." He tossed her a smile and stepped out into another downpour so heavy his flashlight beam barely cut through.

The hug he'd shared with Blair had surprised him. He acted impulsively after seeing the stark fear on her face. Still, the action had been foreign to him. Intimacy was something he ran from. Who would want a man disfigured as he was?

Some called him a hero for running into a burning building to save a woman and her newborn child. Others called him a fool. Maverick wavered between the two. He'd barely made it out alive after being pinned by a falling piece of roof. That was the last time he'd gone out with the volunteer fire department. Every time the call went out, he felt like a coward.

Not seeing anything of interest outside, he returned to the warmth of the fire. The relief on Blair's face when he entered the cabin stopped his heart. He smiled and stood a few feet from the fire.

"You'll warm faster if you come closer." She motioned him over.

"I'm good over here." He wrapped his arms around him and perched on a splintering stool. The cabin would warm enough in a while to chase away the chill. No need to hug the flames.

"Did you see anything?"

He shook his head. "Whoever was out there seems to be gone."

"If Brittney was held on this mountain, where?"

He shrugged. "There are a hundred cabins just like this one. I'm sure once the weather clears, there will be search copters in the air."

"They won't see anything unless she's in the open."

"Still, it's something. In the meantime, we'll keep searching on the ground." One way or the other, dead or alive, they'd eventually find her. He prayed they would find her alive, but that got slimmer with each passing day.

Blair moved to the floor and leaned against Diamond. Soon, her eyes drifted closed as she used the dog for a pillow.

Sleep sounded good, but Maverick wouldn't sleep. Someone had been, or still was, out there. Someone who didn't want to be seen. Whether hunters or someone more evil waited to be determined.

He pulled out his half-empty water bottle from his pack and took a swig. The storm could last a good while and the water would have to wait. The granola bar in his back beckoned as he returned the bottle, but that would have to wait until hunger got worse.

Despite the crackling of the fire that kept him on edge, his eyes grew heavy. His head slumped forward. A log rolled from the chimney onto the hearth, jolting him awake. He grabbed a rusty fire poker and shoved it back where it belonged. A spark flew and landed on the back of his hand. He hissed and drew back.

"How did you get burned?" Blair waved her hand in front of her face.

"A fire."

"Ha, ha. You don't have to tell me if it bothers you. I'm only being nosy."

He sighed. "I was a volunteer fireman for a while. Got caught in a burning house. Two firemen dragged me out, but the damage had been done."

"Must've hurt."

"Yeah." His chest, face, and right shoulder showed exactly how much it had hurt.

"Firemen are real life heroes in my opinion." She sat up and gave Diamond some of her water.

There was that hero word again. "I'd say your job qualifies you as a hero."

A blush rose to her cheeks. "I don't risk my life though."

"You're afraid of the dark yet you came out to find a missing girl."

"It's my job." She ducked her head, her dark hair falling forward and hiding her face.

"Makes you a hero in my eyes." Far more than a man so afraid of fire that he'd sit too far back to get the benefit of the flame's warmth.

"Thank you." She glanced out the window. "The rain is letting up. We should be able to head back soon."

"How do you like the motel?"

"I've stayed in worse."

"Why not stay at the ranch? I'm sure the boss wouldn't mind. There's plenty of room."

"Don't they have visitors a lot?" She turned to face him.

"Sure, but there's plenty of room. A few of the cottages are empty. A couple of the hands have married and moved." Why did he volunteer her to stay on the Rocking W? That would put her right under his nose.

"I'll think about it. It would be closer to where Brittney disappeared." She sat back down next to her dog.

Diamond's ears perked up.

A twig snapped outside.

Maverick pulled his gun and lunged to his feet. "Stay down."

Blair wrapped her arms around the dog's neck, her eyes wide. Growls filled the cabin. "Down girl."

An eerie voice drifted through the open window.

Chapter Six

"Go back!" The voice sang like a taunting nursery rhyme, high and shrill, then repeated itself.

Blair hugged Diamond tighter. What kind of nightmare had they entered?

A cackling laugh followed the taunt, the pounding of feet on rain-soaked ground, then silence for a moment before a piercing howl raised the hair on the back of Blair's neck. Her throat seized.

Maverick put a finger to his lips. After several tense seconds of no more warnings or sounds coming from outside, he jerked his head toward the door. "We need to go. This cabin could be a trap for us."

"You think we're in danger?" She tried to swallow, her spit getting stuck halfway down her throat.

He nodded. "That had the false sound of a recording. Someone is playing games with us, Blair. I don't like it. Not one bit."

Games? What kind of psychotic nutcase toyed with people in the middle of the woods in a thunderstorm?

Maverick opened the door. "Let's go. Stay close."

He didn't have to tell her twice. She'd glue herself

to him if she could. Keeping one hand tight around Diamond's collar, she followed him out.

The rain had stopped, thankfully. The plop of drips off leaves onto a sodden ground was the only sound she heard other than her hoarse breathing.

Her flashlight, once a beacon to light the way, flickered. They'd been out too long. The batteries were dying. "Do we have more batteries?"

"No." Maverick glanced back. "I didn't anticipate being out this long."

Oh, Lord. Her breathing increased as her light sputtered then quit. She banged her palm against the took to no avail.

The air around her thickened. The once beautiful forest teemed with evil that stalked them from the shadows. She dropped the flashlight and bent over, hands on her knees to catch her breath.

"Keep moving, Blair." Maverick took her arm and straightened her. "We need to get back to the horses."

The horses. The poor things had been out in the rain all this time. "They'll be miserable."

"They're fine. In fact, they probably gave up on us, pulled free, and headed home."

"Which means the others are looking for us." Hope leaped in her chest.

"Maybe, but it's more likely that the horses are grazing in the yard waiting for the hands to wake up."

Couldn't he give her some small thing to keep her from losing control? She glared up at him, then stomped back the way they'd come. At least she thought she did.

"This way."

She turned in the opposite direction. This was the

last time she'd head out at night in unfamiliar territory. Different perspective or not, the night had been nothing less than a nightmare.

Another howl rose and Diamond woofed deep in her throat.

Minutes seemed like hours as they trudged through the woods. Humidity pressed down on them like a suffocating blanket. Blair's muscles ached. Fatigue clung to her. Her head sagged.

When they returned to the ranch, she'd crash wherever Maverick said she could and catch a few hours sleep before resuming the search for Brittney under the light of day.

She glanced up in time to see a shadow dart between two trees.

Diamond barked and took off like a rocket.

"Maverick!" Blair gave chase.

"Stay with me, Blair." His call followed her. "Blair!" His voice started to fade.

"Diamond, come!" Blair stopped under a tall pine. "Here, girl."

She glanced around the inky darkness. Her throat seized. Her heart stopped. She couldn't see any sign of Maverick or Diamond. Had she really run that far? Something rustled close by. "Diamond?"

Oh, no. She started to hyperventilate. She'd managed to get herself lost. She turned in a slow circle. Where was Maverick? He could have easily kept up with her. She wasn't a fast runner. Something must have happened to him.

Raw fear blinded her, and she sagged against the tree. Just like that time years ago, she was alone in a strange forest. Only this time a mad man played games.

She dug her weapon from her backpack. Let him, her, them, come for her.

Pulling strength from the very core of her, she did her best to follow the trail of trampled leaves and broken branches she'd left on her wild run after Diamond. The dog would find her. Diamond never strayed too far for too long.

Worry over Maverick tugged at her. She didn't know him well, but she knew him well enough to know he would've been right on her heels if he could.

Fear nagged at her again. What if Maverick lay dead or severely injured? She had no idea how to find him. She would be alone with whoever toyed with them. She wanted to call out to him, call Diamond back, but the dread of letting those who followed them know her location kept her silent.

She needed to find a place to hole up. A hollowed tree or dense brush. Something to provide her an element of protection against the weather and discovery. She had a bit of water in her pack, a granola bar, she could manage until the sun came up. Then, she could find her way back to the road.

Diamond would find her before then. The dog would wait with her, providing not only comfort, but a warning system. "Diamond?" She whispered. Please, God, don't let anything have happened to her best friend.

The forest seemed to come alive the closer morning came. Trees whispered. Blair sagged to the ground, exhaustion winning over the desire to find the road. She plastered her back against a tree and hugged her arms tight around her middle, keeping one hand tightly on her gun.

Her mind started to play tricks on her in the darkness. What if Maverick had deliberately let her get too far ahead of him? What did she really know about him?

Maybe he had something to do with Brittney's disappearance. He did seem a bit casual about the search. At least more so than Blair. Had he led her to the woods, at night, to set a trap?

~

Maverick put a hand to his head. A knot rose on his skull. He hadn't seen the hit coming.

Struggling to his feet, he snatched his cowboy hat from the ground and glanced around for sight of Blair. What had she been thinking running after the dog? Wouldn't Diamond return on her own without a foolish chase through dark woods?

Another feel of the knot, he squared his shoulders and searched the ground for his gun. Whoever had knocked him out had taken it. At least they hadn't killed him. He couldn't say the same about Blair, but he sure hoped she hadn't been harmed.

What if those who had taken Brittney took her? If Brittney had been taken. He still wasn't convinced. Even so, he'd search for the girl until they found her whether they found her alive with friends, held captive, or murdered. Everyone lost deserved to be found.

His head pounded as he trudged in the direction he'd last seen Blair go. As he hiked, he finished the last of his water and ate the granola bar. Sunup was only a couple of hours away. He'd find where they'd tied the horses quick enough then. If the animals had gone, he'd find the road where he'd get cell phone service and call the ranch for a ride.

The hair on the back of his neck rose with each rustle or the snap of a twig. His back tensed, expecting a shot to ring out and a bullet to take him. How could he have let someone get the drop on him?

The dog had barked and taken off, Blair right after her. Maverick made a move to follow…that's the last thing he remembered.

Whoever had hit him had lured the dog away as a decoy. A means to take Maverick off his guard. He shook his head. A rookie move.

Occasionally he stopped moving to listen for the sound of a bark or a call of his name. When only silence reigned, he continued. Blair and the dog could have taken off in any direction. He might be heading further away from them.

Something crashed nearby.

He whirled and broke off a tree branch to use as a weapon.

Diamond, tail wagging, emerged.

"Girl, I almost bashed your head in." He patted her. "Take me to Blair. Can you do that?"

The dog's ears perked, then she turned and loped away.

Ignoring the pounding in his skull, Maverick followed and fought back the nausea roiling in his stomach. He couldn't let the dog out of his sight.

"Diamond!" Blair's cry was the sweetest thing Maverick had heard in a long time.

He parted some low-lying branches and stepped out into where she sat at the base of an oak tree and hugged her dog. "Are you okay?"

She glared over the dog's head. "Where were you?"

"Knocked out on the ground." He put a hand to the back of his head again. "Someone snuck up and clobbered me."

She didn't look convinced at first, then got to her feet. "Let me see." She parted his hair and sucked in a breath. "That's a nasty lump. You might have a concussion."

"Other than a headache and an upset stomach, I'm good. Let's get out of here."

"Do you know the way?"

He glanced upward. The clouds had scattered, leaving the moon and stars to lead the way. "Sure do." They had a couple of hours hike. Hopefully, he wouldn't have to rest too many times and make the night any longer than it had already been.

"I haven't heard anything in a long time," Blair whispered behind him.

"Neither have I. Hopefully that means whoever was tormenting us has gone." He left out that they'd taken his gun. He didn't see any reason to frighten her more than she already was.

Every few minutes, he glanced back to see whether the dog reacted to anything. No ear perks, throaty growls or bristling fur. How had whoever she'd taken off after gotten away?

"Would Diamond have caught up with these people, then left them?"

"No. She'd have barked to alert me and held them. I saw a shadow move right before she took off."

"Human?"

"I think so. It moved pretty fast."

He tucked his tongue into the side of his mouth. A human cannot outrun a dog. So, again, how had they gotten away?" "I want to come take a closer look after grabbing a few hours of sleep."

"Do you think Mr. Wyatt will mind if I crash on the sofa? Heck, at this point, I'd sleep in the barn."

"I'm sure we can find you a bed." He repeated his invitation for her to consider staying on the ranch.

"I'll let you know after I've had some sleep."

He led her to the road. "This is the best thing I've seen all day." He took a deep breath. "I can get a signal to call for a ride now." As he'd expected, the horses had left. He didn't relish another hour's hike which is what it would take to reach the ranch.

River, one of the ranch hands, answered the phone in the bunkhouse. "Sure, dude. I'll be there in a few. I can see the horses milling around outside. You should've tethered them better."

"I didn't see the point in having them waiting in a downpour. See ya." He hung up and turned to Blair. "About twenty minutes."

"Thank goodness." She plopped on a patch of grass. "I'm so tired I don't care if the ground is wet. All I want is a hot shower and some sleep. The order of those two things is negotiable."

He couldn't agree more.

Headlights pierced the dawn. He squinted, recognizing the beat-up truck from the ranch. "Our ride is here."

As he opened the passenger door for Blair, he glanced at the woods. *I'm coming back. When I find you, you'll be the sorry ones.*

Chapter Seven

Blair tossed off the crocheted afghan she'd covered with and glanced at her phone. Ugh. Only four hours of sleep. After the night she'd had with Maverick, she definitely needed much more.

"Good. You're awake." Maverick entered the living room and handed her a cup of coffee.

"You're chipper with only a few hours of sleep. Thanks." She wrapped her hands around the cup and breathed deep of the rich aroma.

"Slept like a baby for four hours. That's all I need." He perched on a chair opposite her. "The boss said you can rent one of the cottages for as long as you need."

"I'll take him up on it." For a man who didn't like conversation, he sure talked a lot in the morning.

"I know you wanted to head back out and search for tracks in the light. We also need to let the sheriff know about seeing lights in the woods." He took a big gulp of his drink and got to his feet. "Breakfast is ready. We'll leave right after."

She wanted a shower more than food, but that didn't seem an option. Heaving a sigh, she followed him to the kitchen where a handful of men in jeans and boots already sat around the table.

Maverick made introductions, Blair mumbled something she hoped was a coherent greeting, then took the seat offered her.

Before she could blink a heaping plate of pancakes was set in front of her. Someone passed a bottle of syrup. Her stomach rumbled reminding her it had been a long time since she'd eaten anything other than a granola bar, which she'd scarfed down on the way to the ranch.

The conversation around the table focused on ranch things, thankfully, leaving her to eat in silence and wake up. After eating only two of the pancakes, she pushed back her chair and stood. "I'm ready."

Maverick frowned. "I'm still eating." The man was on his second plate full.

"Is it alright if I shower while you finish?"

"Absolutely." The cook motioned for her to follow. "I'll show you the way and get you a towel."

"You're a life saver." Blair smiled. A shower would finish waking her up so she could face the day.

"I'll fill a thermos with coffee and pack a lunch. You and Maverick might be working all day." She opened a hall closet and pulled out a fluffy towel. "Shower is right in there. I'll hurry the man up so y'all can get started. Thank you for trying to find Brittney."

"You're welcome." Blair smiled and closed the bathroom door.

When she'd finished, she joined Maverick on the sweeping front porch. He stopped his conversation with Wyatt and faced her. "We'll fetch your things from the motel, then stop at the sheriff's office. It's fine if you leave the dog here."

"Diamond goes everywhere with me." She waved for the dog to stop sniffing around a bush and come to her side. To leave her best friend behind was unheard of.

Maverick shrugged. "I'll drive." With long strides he reached his truck and opened the passenger side door.

Diamond jumped in first and climbed into the backseat. Blair settled into the front passenger seat. "There really isn't a need to open doors for me. I'm capable."

"My mama would come out of the grave and whoop me." He grinned, then jogged to the driver's side.

Not only a cowboy, but a gentleman as well. She clicked her seatbelt into place and settled back for the drive down the mountain.

At the motel, she threw the few things she'd brought with her into her bag, then headed to the office to pay what she owed. She'd been reluctant to stay on the ranch, but the cottage a little ways from the house would still give her the independence she enjoyed. Finished, she joined Maverick back in the truck.

"We really don't have much to tell the sheriff."

"No, but he should know there is someone wandering around at night. Not to mention the recordings and hitting me in the back of the head. That's enough." He backed from the parking spot.

Less than five minutes later, he pulled in front of the red brick building that housed the sheriff's department. "This won't take long."

"I'm not worried about the time as long as we

aren't in the woods again at night." She shuddered.

"I promise we'll return to the ranch before nightfall."

She exited the truck before he could open her door. Ignoring his frown, she marched into the building, Diamond at her side.

"Good morning, Maverick." The receptionist smiled. "Need to speak to Sheriff Westbrook?"

"Yes, ma'am."

"I'll let him know you're here." She spoke into the phone on her desk, then ushered them down the hall.

The sheriff stood when they entered his office and extended a hand, first to Maverick, then to Blair. "Good morning. What can I do for you?" He listened quietly as Maverick filled him in on the night before. His features formed hard lines. "I don't like those kind of pranks. No more investigating at night. Obviously, whoever took Brittney is still in town. That's the only good news to come out of your story."

"Good news?" Blair tilted her head.

"Means she isn't far away." The sheriff folded his hands on his desk. "If they'd taken her away from here, they wouldn't be hanging around."

"Unless they're here to snatch another girl."

He narrowed his eyes. "You're thinking trafficking?"

"It's a strong possibility." She crossed her arms. "It's running rampant in the country. No need to think it hadn't come to Misty Hollow."

"I sure hope you're wrong, ma'am. We've got a chopper going up in a few hours. Maybe we'll get lucky."

So did she, but it was something they needed to strongly consider.

~

After filing a complaint with the sheriff, Maverick drove them back to where they'd searched the night before. It would be hard to find the tracks, but once they located the cabin, he should be able to pick up the trail.

Trafficking? He sure hoped not. Misty Hollow had already dealt with that particular evil... among others. Yep, this town had had its share of trouble and then some.

He parked the truck on the side of the road, got out, and fetched the bag Mrs. White had packed from the back seat. He eyed the dog who wagged her tail, then gave him a lick on the face before he could back up.

Blair laughed. "She likes you."

"We've been spending enough time together." He gave the dog a look that dared it to lick him again, then closed the door as she bounded out Blair's open door.

"Why don't you like dogs?" Blair frowned. "I don't trust people who don't like dogs."

"Then we have a problem." He returned her stare with a hard one of his own. "We have to trust each other, and it isn't that I don't like dogs, but a German Shepherd bit me when I was a kid, and I've been leery ever since." He slammed his door closed.

"She won't bite unless ordered or I'm being threatened."

"Then I'm safe." He hoped. He had no intention of harming Blair. Making her angry was something they'd have to wait and see about.

He hefted the backpack onto his shoulders and headed into the woods. This time, he'd lead the way instead of the dog. If they found evidence of Brittney, it would be a bonus. Right now, he wanted a clue as to who had hit him. He might very well ask Blair to sic her dog on them if he found them. His head still ached from the blow.

The previous night's rain helped muffle their footsteps. He didn't expect his attacker to still be out there but planned on being vigilant anyway. He patted the gun on his hip and hoped he wouldn't have a reason to use it.

It took a little over an hour to reach the cabin. Things inside looked exactly as they'd left with extra ashes in the fireplace and footprints in the dust. He headed around the building not finding anything other than his prints and Blair's…wait a minute. There. A partial muddy print near the glassless window.

A nail protruded from the frame. Where the recorder had been hung?

Blair stepped next to him and took a picture with her phone. "We might need photos for the sheriff."

"Good thinking." Another stroll around the perimeter didn't show anything new.

He moved back to the window and searched for footprints heading away from the cabin. Last night's rain made tracking easy. He spotted the occasional print where dead leaves had been scuffed to the side.

"If we had something for Diamond to smell, she'd lead us right to them." Blair snapped another picture.

"If we find whoever "they" are, we'll find Brittney." Head down, he continued following the tracks, pausing where he'd fallen and studying the area.

Whoever hit him had hid behind a tree. Most likely the ancient pine close to the trail. Its trunk was wide enough for someone to hide behind. There was the spot where he'd hit the ground. There were the footprints of whoever hit him.

He studied the almost perfect print in the mud. A zig-zag pattern he'd seen before. His heart dropped. A pattern common among the youth of Misty Hollow.

"What's wrong?"

He straightened. "I think we're dealing with kids."

She took another photo. "Vince Matterson."

"Don't make accusations without proof." But they should pay a visit to the high school and look at the kid's shoes.

"What do you know about him?"

"Nothing." He didn't have a need to hang out with high school students. "Star quarterback. Popular. Hard worker during the summer. He's worked on the ranch the last two summers. That's it. Dylan might know more."

They continued following those tracks, plus two more with the same sole pattern until they stopped at the road. They'd made a circle and came out of the woods about half a mile farther down from where he'd packed the truck.

"Guess we walk from here." Blair turned and headed in the direction they'd started.

A chopper thumped overhead, flying low. The pilot tipped his baseball hat and rose higher in the sky.

"Guess we aren't a threat." Blair grinned over her shoulder.

"Nope." At least the search from the air had started. When they returned to the ranch, he'd get a map of the area and circle as many of the hunting cabins as he could remember locations. Then, they'd search each and every one for signs of the missing girl. After that, he had no idea of their next step.

"It's lunch time." Blair stopped next to his truck. "Let's eat, then have Diamond start a search from where we found those tire tracks. I doubt she can pick up the trail after the rain, but since we're already out here, I'd like to try."

"Okay. After that, we pay a visit to the high school." Maverick intended to find some more answers before calling it a day. How much authority did he have as a temporary deputy? Could he ask for cell phones to be handed over? Bring someone in for questioning?

If he didn't know, the person most likely wouldn't either. He could intimidate them and face whatever consequences afterward for his actions.

Someone had played games with them last night, hit him in the head, and he wanted to know who. He was willing to risk a reprimand from the sheriff in order to get those answers.

~

We have to stop the woman and her dog. However possible. And it's time to take another girl. Earn the money I send you.

He grinned and closed the text message before slipping the phone into the pocket of his jeans. The abduction, the luring, was his favorite part.

Chapter Eight

Blair wanted to slap the arrogant grin from Vince's face and wished Maverick had been able to come with her. But a pregnant mare had required his attention on the ranch.

The first thing she'd done when Vince entered the room was glance at his shoes. The proper tread, but no mud. "Where were you last night between ten p.m. and one a.m.?"

"Asleep. Ask my parents." He crossed muscled arms.

"We will." Teenagers snuck out at night. She had. She folded her hands on the tabletop in the school's conference room and speared him with her sternest glare. "The problem here is that I don't believe you."

"That's your prerogative." He shrugged. "Why would I take the girl I wanted to date? By taking her, I'd never have a chance to date the prettiest girl in school."

"Revenge? After all, she wanted nothing to do with you. Take her out of the equation and move on."

"That's pretty far-fetched. Look." He matched her posture. "Unless you've got evidence I had something to do with her going missing, I need to get back to class. I have a test to take. If I don't keep my grades up, I'll get kicked off the team."

She wouldn't get anything out of him. "Fine, but I may have more questions at another time."

He stood and sneered. "You're not even a cop."

"Ex-cop here with the sheriff's permission. It wouldn't take much to have one of his deputies haul you in to be questioned there." She smiled. "I bet that would look really good on your college application."

He muttered a derogatory word for her and stormed from the room. Seconds later, another boy, less arrogant, entered and sat. Fear flickered in his eyes.

Blair glanced at the list in front of her. "Jacob Warren?"

"Yes, ma'am."

He answered the questions same as Vince had, just as the next kid, Billy Wilson. The last of what the other students said were part of Vince's group, entered. "You must be Jacob Warren."

The boy nodded, keeping his head down. "Am I in trouble?"

"That's up to you." She fired the same questions at him, taking note how his squirming increased with each one. "Look Jacob. A nice girl is missing. Surely, if it was your sister, you'd want someone to cooperate and find her. Wouldn't you?"

"How do you know I have a sister?"

Lucky guess. Blair kept the smile on her face. Maybe she'd get somewhere with this one. "Do you know something? This room is a safe place, Jacob. You can tell me. The authorities won't know where the information came from."

"Those who took her will know."

"So, you do know where she is?"

"I've only heard whispered rumors."

"Do you know where Brittney Pitts is?"

"I might."

"Do you know who took her?"

He shook his head hard enough to cause a curl to flop over his forehead. "Like I said, I've only heard where she might be. A few of the players say they saw her." He refused to give names.

"So…" She sat against the chair back. "Some of your friends know where she is and said nothing?"

"Scared, probably."

Right. She didn't believe that for a red-hot second. "Tell me where she is, Jacob."

He took a deep, shuddering breath. "There's an old barn out on 64. It has a faded American flag painted on the side of it. No one has used that barn in a very long time. That's where they said she was."

"Is she alive?"

"Last I heard."

Blair got to her feet. "You've been a big help, Jacob. Thank you. You might very well have saved Brittney's life."

"You'll leave my name out of this?"

"Promise." She swept up her notes and marched out of the building.

Maverick sat in his truck next to her rental. "The mare is going to birth her foal just fine."

"I know where Brittney is."

"Really?" He reached over and thrust open the passenger side door. "Get in. Let's go get that girl."

As usual, Diamond jumped in first. Blair climbed

into the seat. "I'll call the sheriff's office while we drive." She described the barn. "Do you know it?"

"Sure do." He pressed the accelerator, rocketing them from the parking lot and onto the highway. "We should be there in fifteen minutes. Good work, Blair."

Her face heated. "I got lucky in questioning the right kid." She didn't know why his approval mattered, but it did.

She dialed the sheriff's department and received word that they would meet her and Maverick at the barn. Hope leaped in her heart. They were going to save Brittney. Her job in Misty Hollow would be over.

She cut a sideways glance at Maverick's strong profile. Strange, but she'd miss the cowboy. Despite his occasional surliness, they worked well together. Not to mention how handsome he was. It had been a long time since a man had treated her with the care he had, especially when comforting her about her fear of the dark.

"Mud on my face?" He quirked a brow.

"No, just thinking how my time here is almost over."

"Going to miss Misty Hollow?"

"I haven't really had a chance to get to know the place."

"Maybe you should stick around for a few days. Take a little vacation. You've earned one."

Maybe she would. She did like to take a few days off after each job.

Her thoughts quieted as Maverick pulled off the highway and into weeds and grass that scratched the underbelly of the truck. No vehicles had gone that way in a long time. What if Jacob had sent them on a wild goose chase? She'd wring his thick football playing neck if he had.

"Armed?" Maverick reached for his door handle.

"Yes." She exited the truck and waited for Diamond. "Stay close, girl."

Sandwiched between her dog and Maverick, Blair moved through the thigh high grass toward a barn sitting silent in the afternoon. The gaping windows resembled malevolent eyes beckoning her into the devil's lair. *Please, God, let Brittney be alive.*

Maverick put a finger to his lips and plastered his back to the barn wall.

Blair copied.

Diamond woofed deep in her throat.

Maverick whirled, gun at the ready, and stepped into the barn.

~

Despite it being the middle of the day, the interior of the barn sat in deep shadow. No animals announced their presence. A bird flew from one of the rafters overhead, sending Maverick's heart into his throat.

"It's empty." Blair's words, hoarse and deep, sounded loud to his ears.

"There are stalls to check." He moved forward, taking care in the placement of each step. If someone was lying in wait, he didn't want to announce their presence any more than they already had. He put a finger to his lips again and motioned for Blair to check the stalls on their right while he took the ones on the left.

He found nothing until he reached the fourth of the five stalls on his side of the barn. Brittney sat in a pile of dirty hay, bound and gagged. Next to her was an empty water bottle and the crust of a sandwich on an otherwise empty paper plate.

"Shh, darlin'. I'm here to help you." He reached for the blindfold. "Blair, over here!" He then removed the gag and untied her hands and feet. "Are you hurt?"

Tears streaming down her face, the girl shook her head.

"Brittney Pitts?" Blair asked from behind him.

"Yes. I want to go home."

"That's where we're taking you." Maverick helped her to her feet. "Can you tell us how you got here?"

"I was walking to the bus stop when two guys in skull masks jumped from the bushes and grabbed me. They stuck a needle in my neck. The next thing I knew I was in a cabin on the mountain. After a day or two…I don't know how long…they brought me here." Her words broke on a sob. "They were going to hand me over to someone else tonight."

Then they'd found her just in time. "You didn't recognize the ones who took you?"

"They never came without the mask, and they disguised their voices." She ducked her head.

Maverick frowned. Something about her story didn't feel right. "Are you sure? Even with masks, you'd know the shape of them if you'd met them."

"I'm sure!" She covered her face with her hands. "I want to go home."

Diamond nudged the girl with her snout.

Brittney wrapped her arms around the dog's neck. "I have a dog. I miss my dog."

Maverick met Blair's concerned glance over the girl's head. "Any other questions?"

"No. Let's take her home."

The moment they stepped from the barn, the sheriff's car pulled up. Westbrook got out. "She's okay?"

"We're taking her home. She seems fine." Even though Maverick believed she lied about her abducted her. She knew them but was too afraid to say.

"We'll take her to the station and let her folks come for her so we can take a statement. You two come in today or tomorrow to fill out a statement." He held out a hand. "This way, Brittney."

She cast a glance at Maverick, then Blair. "Thank you."

He nodded and watched until the sheriff had her in the back of his car. "She knows who took her."

"I got that feeling, too, but if she won't talk, there isn't anything we can do." Blair headed for the truck.

"Let me buy you supper," he said climbing into the driver's seat. "Payment for a job well done. We found her safe and alive."

"Because someone had a conscience." She turned in her seat. "Jacob also knows who took her but is too afraid to say. Someone has a tight hold on the teens of this town. I wish I could stick around to find out who."

"Why don't you?"

"That isn't my job. Search and rescue is, and supper sounds wonderful."

Tomorrow life would return to normal, and Blair would be gone. His heart dropped a little. She might've been the one. The woman he could see spending the rest of his life with. A woman not repulsed by his scars. A brave, strong woman he could see working at his side. He could enter into search and rescue with her.

They'd be a team. If she weren't leaving.

At the diner, they both ordered the chicken fried chicken special. Maverick could see Diamond tied up outside enjoying a steak. Lucy always did take care of any animals brought to her diner even though she didn't allow them inside. Animals always ate free.

"How do you feel?" He cut into his chicken.

"About finding Brittney? Relieved." She smiled. "It's a thousand times better than the alternative."

"How do you deal when you find one deceased?"

She sobered. "I cry myself to sleep for a few nights."

"You won't have to this time." He reached across the table and patted her hand. "You can sleep like a baby in the cottage."

"Will Mr. Wyatt let me stay another night or two if I want to do a little sightseeing in Misty Hollow?"

"You're paying rent, so I don't see why not." He'd get to spend a few more days with her in town. "I can show you the mist over the valley if you get up early enough one morning. It's how the town got its name. I think it's one of the most beautiful sights I've ever seen."

"I'd like that." She stiffened as she glanced out the window. "The sheriff is coming, and he doesn't look happy."

Maverick followed her gaze. "Nope." The sheriff looked steaming mad. He wasn't here with good news.

Chapter Nine

Sheriff Westbrook stopped at their table and removed his hat. "Looks like you're sticking around for a while, Miss. Oakley. We've had another girl disappear."

"What?"

"Lesley Beane. She isn't a cheerleader or part of that so-called popular group. She's a young woman who lives with a poor family in a shack outside of town and stays to herself. She never made it to lunch today. Checked into her morning classes, then poof by lunchtime."

Blair shot a concerned glance at Maverick. "I was just there talking to the football players." If she had the boys occupied, then they couldn't be the ones who took Lesley. She'd been wrong the whole time and now another girl was in danger.

"She disappeared from the school?" Maverick frowned.

"Appears that way." The sheriff slapped his hat back on his head. "If the two of you could head to the school when you've eaten, I'd appreciate it."

Appetite gone, Blair pushed aside the uneaten

portion of her meal and stood. "I'm ready now." They had no time to waste.

Maverick shoveled in another big mouthful, grabbed his hat off the seat next to him, and followed Blair from the diner.

Mr. White met them in the parking lot holding a black backpack adorned with white polka dots. "This is Lesley's. I figured the dog might need it in order to get a track."

"Unless she left in a vehicle." Blair took the pack. "Thanks. Does the school have cameras?"

"No. We're too small for that." He took a deep breath through his nose, then exhaled slowly. "This isn't like Lesley, any more than it was Brittney. Too different walks of life, but both responsible girls. Lesley is a straight A student." He fished a photo from the pocket of his shirt. "Here is this year's school picture."

Blair studied the pretty face of a girl with red hair and freckles. Not a speck of makeup. Shyness and intelligence shined from nut brown eyes. Just as pretty as Brittney in her own way. "Someone led us to Brittney. Let's talk to him again about Lesley."

Mr. White blinked, long and slow. "One of my students knew where Brittney was?"

"Yes, sir, but I promised to keep his identity a secret. I guess that's a moot point now, but his name goes no farther than the three of us. I need to speak to Jacob Warren."

"I'll have him paged to my office, then I'll send him to the conference room." He shook his head. "I don't see how you can keep his identity a secret now."

She didn't either. "We'll have to get protection for the boy." Whether his buddies were responsible or not,

Jacob knew things. Things that could get him into a lot of trouble.

Followed by Maverick and Diamond, Blair headed for the conference room while the school principal returned to his office. Less than ten minutes later, a pale Jacob entered the conference room.

"I heard you found Brittney." He plopped into a chair. "Are you trying to get me killed?"

Blair narrowed her eyes. "Why do you think someone wants to kill you?"

"That's the kind of people you're dealing with." His eyes darted to Maverick, then back to her. "This isn't a game, lady."

"I don't believe it is." She stiffened. "What do you know about Lesley Beane?"

"Who?" His brow furrowed.

Blair slid the girl's photo across the table. "She went missing by lunchtime. Right from school property."

"I don't know her, I swear." Fear, raw and naked, settled on his face.

"Brittney said she was first held in a cabin on the mountain. Do you happen to know which cabin?"

He swallowed, his Adam's apple bobbing. "Please. You don't know what you're asking."

"I know a girl's life is at stake."

"Look, son." Maverick leaned closer. "We can get the sheriff's department to protect you. It's imperative that you tell us where this girl is if you have any inkling at all."

"All I know is where Brittney was held. Do you know the old Hammons cabin?"

Maverick gave a slow nod.

"That's where Brittney was taken first."

"Who took her?"

He shook his head so hard, Blair thought he'd give himself a neck ache. "I can't tell you. Please."

Sheriff Westbrook opened the door and stepped inside. "This your informant?"

Jacob jumped to his feet. "You arresting me?"

"Taking you in for questioning."

"I'm a dead man." The boy covered his face with his hands. "I'm telling you I don't know who is behind all this. I only know they mean business."

"Come on." The sheriff took the boy by the arm. "Good work, Miss Oakley. Maverick."

"We're heading to the Hammons cabin." Blair stood. "It would be nice if you could send backup."

"I'll do that as soon as I get in the car with this guy. I'll also be placing a call to the FBI. Again."

Heads in the front office turned as they all trooped outside, one of them Vince's who held a cell phone to his ear. Blair stopped and faced the boy. Neither backed down until Maverick called her name. Blair put two fingers to her eyes, then at the boy to let him know she was watching him before following Maverick to his truck.

"I think your first instinct was right." Maverick backed from the parking spot. "We're dealing with a ring. My question is...why did it take so long for Brittney to be shipped away from Misty Hollow?"

"Good question." In Blair's experience, girls were moved very quickly in order to avoid detection. "There's one thing I'm sure of. That someone in Misty Hollow, other than that group of football players, is involved. Teenagers don't have the mental capacity to head up a ring."

"They're used to lure the girls?"

"Usually. Get a goodlooking boy to come onto a girl, convince her to meet him somewhere, and...well, she's gone."

"What's the success rate of finding a trafficking victim?"

"Not very good. It's much easier if they go missing on their own."

~

By the time they hit the highway, traffic had come to a standstill. Maverick whipped the steering wheel to the right and sped down the shoulder.

Blair gripped the handle above her head. "This is not a good idea."

"Time is of the essence." He increased their speed and rocketed down the next exit ramp. "Too bad we don't have a light and siren to make other drivers get out of our way."

"How far is this cabin?"

"Once we get to the top of the mountain, we have a thirty-minute hike." He prayed they'd reach the cabin before the girl was moved.

"She won't be there."

"You don't know that."

"I feel it."

"Let's hope you're wrong."

"I thought maybe the football players were innocent after all, but Jacob knows too much for that to be true. What I don't know is how involved are they?"

He cut her a quick glance as he took the turnoff for the mountain road. "That's what we need to find out." And they would. He wouldn't stop until they had all the answers they needed. He would not fail these girls.

Redemption for past failures. Yes, he'd saved the family in the fire, but he'd failed a young woman and her child while deployed. No matter how fast he'd moved, it hadn't been enough to rescue them before their captors killed them. He could not let that happen again.

He reached for Blair's hand. "We'll find her."

She nodded, keeping her gaze out the window. "Yes."

She didn't sound convinced.

Maverick sighed and pulled onto the old logging road. Before they reached the place he'd parked the truck the night they'd taken cover from the rain, he stopped. "We get out here."

"Let's go to work, girl." Blair climbed from the truck and held Lesley's backpack out to Diamond. "Find."

The dog sniffed, barked, and put her snout to the ground. After a minute, she took off into the trees.

"We'd better run to catch up to her." Blair sprinted after Diamond, Maverick on her heels.

The Hammons cabin didn't sit as deep into the woods as the previous one. Faint footprints, two large, one small, led to the cabin door.

Maverick withdrew his weapon. "Stay behind me."

"Diamond, come."

Taking a deep breath, Maverick approached the cabin, stopping outside to peer in the window. An empty water bottle lay on its side on the dirt floor. No persons were there. "They're gone."

"Diamond, find."

The dog resumed her search, heading west.

"I think she's headed toward the barn." Blair shot Maverick a hopeful glance. "Could they have moved her this fast?"

"If someone told them we were on our way. That Jacob talked." He increased his speed and chased after the dog. Could they get lucky again? Lesley hadn't been missing more than a couple of hours.

Occasionally, Maverick spotted a track, but didn't stop to investigate. The dog was on the scent, and he needed to keep the animal in sight. Behind him, Blair breathed heavily, but didn't complain.

When the barn came into view, Maverick held up a fist to stop her. "Call the dog," he whispered.

"Diamond, come."

The dog followed her command. The three of them stared at the barn for a few minutes. When no one entered or exited, Maverick waved them forward. "Stay close and quiet."

"I know the drill."

"Sorry." He didn't mean to tell her how to do her job. Leading a group of men in rescue missions overseas had left habits hard to break.

As before, he stopped at the door and peered inside. No sound came to him. He stepped inside, gun at the ready.

A bucket lay overturned. A rake on its side. Things that weren't displaced the last time they were there. Evidence someone had been there. That someone still used the barn.

He wracked his mind to come up with an owner's name. Nothing. The sheriff's department should be able to find out and the owner questioned.

They found a frightened Lesley in the same stall they'd found Brittney. Blair rushed forward and removed the girl's gag and blind fold. "We've got you, sweetie."

"Can you tell us who took you?" Maverick stepped forward.

The girl's eyes opened in fright.

He put his gun away and held out his hands. "Don't be scared. We're here to take you home."

"Are my parents okay?" She glanced from him to Blair. "I got a note at school that said I needed to come home right away. I hadn't walked but a block when a van pulled up, two guys got out and put a pillowcase over my head, then shoved me inside. The next thing I knew I woke up in a cabin. Then, they moved me here."

"Where are they now?"

She shook her head. "I don't know. I heard them say they had to get out right away and that someone else would come for me. I thought you were that someone."

"Let's get you out of here before they come." Blair cut her bindings and helped her to her feet.

Maverick studied the terrain outside. Convinced they were alone, he ushered them out. Where was the sheriff? "We've got quite a hike to the road. Help is coming, Lesley."

"My parents?"

"I'm sure they're fine." Blair put an arm around her shoulders. "The note was just a ploy."

Tears poured down the girl's dusty face. "Why? I'm new to the school. I don't know anyone. Why would someone want to hurt me?"

"We're going to find out," Maverick said. "There's the cavalry."

Two squad cars pulled up to the barn. The sheriff got out of one and marched toward them. "Sorry. We got another call. Maverick?" He jerked his head to the side. "I need to talk to you. Miss Oakley, Lesley, we'll be right back."

"What's up, sheriff?" Maverick's heart dropped at the stern look on the sheriff's face. The same look he'd had when he'd notified them of Lesley's disappearance.

"We never got Jacob safely to the office. He jumped from the car when we got stalled in traffic. His body has been found in the lake. We're headed that way. Deputy Hudson will take Lesley to the office until her parents can come for her."

Maverick glanced back at Blair. Jacob was dead.

Chapter Ten

This was her fault. Blair's breath hitched as the sheriff repeated himself. If she hadn't pressured the boy...

"This isn't on you." Maverick's quiet words did nothing to reassure her. "We saved two girls because of you talking to Jacob."

"And a young man is dead." She bent over, hands on her knees to steady her breathing. Diamond whined and nudged her hand.

"You okay to go on, Miss Oakley?" The sheriff asked. "I'd like the owner of this barn questioned, a man by the name of Hubert Grimes, and no one is answering at Lesley's home. If you two can do those two things, I can head back to the lake. Deputy Hudson will secure the crime scene here. The FBI should arrive later today."

She forced herself to stand upright. "I can do this."

Gratitude shined in his eyes. "Good. Let's meet back at the office at six p.m. to fill the FBI in on what we know." With a nod and the tap of his fingers against the brim of his hat, he turned and marched back to his car.

"You sure you're up to this?" Maverick's soft gaze landed on hers. "I can go alone if you need time to process."

"I'll process once we have Jacob's killer behind bars." And those responsible for the abductions. "Where to first?"

"If you need some time—"

"I said I'm fine." She yanked the door open to his truck and climbed in barely giving Diamond time to get in the back. This was her job. She always got the job done. When it was over, then she'd collapse, but not before.

The drive back to town was silent. Blair kept her gaze focused on the landscape. Catching sight of Brittney and her father strolling down the sidewalk, she straightened. The girl walked head down, hoodie covering her head and face, shoulders slumped. "Pull over."

"What do you see?"

"Brittney is heading into the coffee shop." Her father entered the drug store. "I want to talk to her. Hurry. Before her father joins her." She had her door open before the truck stopped. "Keep an eye on Diamond."

She rushed into the shop and got in line behind Brittney. When the girl ordered, Blair ordered for herself and Maverick, then joined the girl off to the side to wait.

"Hey, Brittney."

"Hey," the girl mumbled.

"You doing okay? Back to school?"

"I'm doing online schooling."

"That makes sense." Blair bent to peer under the girl's hood. "You okay?"

She nodded.

"I bet your parents are glad to have you home."

Brittney shrugged. "I'm a prisoner now."

"I'm sure they're only being protective."

The girl glanced up. Her eyes widened. "I've got to go. Dad's waiting." She snatched her order from the counter and rushed outside.

Blair turned and met the stern stare of Mr. Pitts. After several tense seconds, he resumed his walk down the sidewalk, one arm around his daughter's shoulders. Brittney cast a worried glance at Blair, then ducked her head.

Something was very wrong between those two.

The barista called her name a few times before it registered.

"Sorry." Blair grabbed her order and returned to the truck. "Coffee?"

"Thanks. What was that all about?" He set his drink in the cupholder in the console.

"Just a feeling, but Brittney seems afraid of her father. Said they're keeping her a prisoner." She took a sip of her cold, blended drink.

"I'm sure they're worried about all that's going on."

"Maybe, but I think it's more than that."

"A feeling?" He quirked a brow and smiled.

"Smirk all you want, but I've learned to trust those feelings. Do you know where this Hubert Grimes lives?"

"I made a couple of calls while you were inside

and got an address." He pulled the truck away from the curb. "He's a retired farmer and has a house just outside of town. Lives there with his wife, Norma. We'll be there in ten minutes."

Why would Brittney be afraid of her father? With her safe return, the Pitts should be one happy family. "We should question Mrs. Pitts in addition to Grimes and Lesley's parents."

"Okay." Maverick turned onto a curving gravel drive.

A modest ranch-style home with siding that looked like fake bricks sat between two huge magnolia trees. A mixed-breed dog stretched on the front porch, then loped toward them.

"Stay, Diamond." Blair slowly opened her door. When all the dog did was wag its tail, she stood on the gravel drive.

A man in tan coveralls stepped from the house onto the porch. "Welcome."

"You Mr. Grimes?" Maverick moved to Blair's side.

"I am."

Maverick introduced them. "Mind if we ask you a few questions on behalf of the sheriff's department?"

"Not at all. Come on inside. Wife has coffee on." He stepped aside and held the door open. Spotting Diamond, he said, "The dog is welcome. Brutus here won't mind the company."

Blair returned to the truck to let Diamond out. "Good girl."

Inside, the aroma of fresh brewed coffee greeted them. She declined when offered one, while Maverick accepted and sat on the red and green plaid sofa. Blair took a seat next to him while Diamond lay at her feet.

Mr. and Mrs. Grimes sat in chairs across from them. "What do you need to know?"

Blair took a deep breath. There wasn't any need to beat around the bush. "Were you aware that your barn was being used to traffick young girls? It was used to hold two of them over the span of a few days."

Mrs. Grimes gasped and put a hand to her throat. "Hubert?"

"I had no idea. We just returned from a trip to Europe. Something we worked our whole lives for. Only got back yesterday. I haven't been out to that barn yet. Got plans on selling the land."

"Someone was using it. A pitchfork and bucket was moved." Maverick sipped his coffee.

"Well, I don't know anything about that. I'm guess those scoundrels who took the girls were nosing around." He shook his head. "This is terrible. Are the girls okay?"

"Both girls have been rescued." Blair leaned forward. Both of them seemed genuinely surprised and horrified at what their barn had been used for. "If you hear of anything that might be pertinent to their abduction, please give the sheriff's office a call."

Mr. Grimes stood. "You can count on it. I will pray you catch those responsible. I don't know about this world we live in anymore."

"Thank you for your time." Blair got to her feet. They'd learned nothing other than that the Grimes' seemed to have nothing to do with Brittney or Lesley. She thought it prudent to leave out the murder of Jacob Warren.

Back in the truck, Maverick glanced at his phone.

"Sheriff says it doesn't look like foul play regarding Jacob. He thinks the boy might've committed suicide."

Blair jerked. "No way." Could it be true? She refused to believe so. The boy had been frightened, filled with guilt, but to drown himself? No. There were easier ways to commit suicide.

~

"He also said Jacob left his shoes on the shore. Tread matches the prints we found in the woods." He dropped his phone into the middle console. Suicide? Nah, too easy. "The Pitts' place is closer than the place the Beanes rent. We'll stop there first."

The rental the Beanes lived in barely looked habitable. Missing shingles on the roof, a sagging porch, plywood over two of the windows. He glanced at the address on his phone. This was the place.

It took several long knocks before a woman in a soiled nightgown answered the door. Red eyes with dilated pupils peered out. "We ain't buying anything."

"Mrs. Beane? I'm with the sheriff's department. This is Blair Oakley with Arkansas Search and Rescue. Were you aware that your daughter Lesley was missing?"

"What? Dick, did you know Lesley was missing?"

"Ain't seen her in a day or two. Figured she was staying with a friend." The man's slurred words drifted through the open door.

Maverick wanted to slug them both. "Lesley was abducted. She is now at the sheriff's office waiting for one of you to pick her up and bring her home."

Mrs. Beane blinked rapidly. "Can't someone bring her to us? We ain't in no condition to go get her. Don't have a car, either. At least one that works anyway."

Blair made a disgusted noise in her throat. "Your daughter needs her parents right now. Aren't you going to ask whether she's alright?"

"Is she?"

"Yes." Blair frowned.

"That's my girl. She's tough. Quiet, but tough as concrete. Ain't that right, Dick?"

"Yep."

Maverick narrowed his eyes. The woman didn't seem the least bit concerned about her daughter. "You wouldn't know who would've taken her, do you?"

She shook her head hard enough to cause what was left in the bun to fall loose. "Nope. Dick?"

"Nope. Close the door, Ruth. You're letting the hot air in."

Blair's mouth fell open. "Of all the irresponsible—"

"Thank you for your time." He gripped Blair's arm and led her back to the truck. "We won't get anything out of those two."

"Lesley cannot go back to that place. They are either high or drunk and couldn't care a bit that their daughter had been in danger of disappearing forever." She slapped the hood of the truck.

He glanced back at the house in time to see the faded curtains in one window twitch into place. Blair wasn't the only one who listened to her feelings. At that moment, his told him something wasn't right at the Beane home.

"Maybe we'll learn something at the Pitts' place." He climbed into the driver's seat. Another glance at the house showed Mrs. Beane peering out again. Definitely something not right there and warranted further investigating.

"What are you thinking?" Blair asked.

"Did they seem surprised to hear about Lesley?"

"No. Do you think they knew?"

He hated to admit it, but yes. "What if, and this is a long shot, but what if someone offered them money for their daughter? Lesley got a note at school telling her to come home. It had to sound like it came from her parents or she wouldn't have gone, right?"

"She might have. I'm sure one of the women in the front office took the message. It would've been written in her handwriting."

"Unless the message came via text from a parent's cell phone."

"I'll call the school and ask while you drive to the Pitts place." She fished her phone from her pocket. A minute later, she nodded. "No call through the office. This is too horrible to contemplate, Maverick."

"But it does warrant thinking about." He pulled up to a two-story red brick house with white columns. "Bank manager seems to pay well."

"Let's hope we find out something concrete here."

A few minutes later, they sat in a stylish living room across from a bored, but pretty blond woman with a botoxed face. "I'm not sure what I can tell you other than I'm so relieved to have my daughter home with me."

"Is she with your husband now?" Blair raised a brow.

"Yes. He's been taking her to work with him. She uses one of the office computers to do her schoolwork." She gave a sad smile. "My husband is afraid to let her out of his sight."

"What's their relationship like?" Maverick sat back doing his best to look relaxed and feeling as if he failed. Again, his nerves tingled with suspicion.

The woman's eyes focused somewhere over his shoulder. "That's a strange question."

"Not really considering the circumstances."

A small fuzzy dog leaped onto her lap. She absently petted it. "They get along as well as any parent and teenager, I guess. They argue, but my husband loves our daughter very much."

"And you, ma'am?"

She bolted to her feet. "I think it's time the two of you left. I'm still not over the trauma of what…could have happened."

"Did happen," Blair interjected. "Your daughter was kidnapped, Mrs. Pitts, with the intention of shipping her away for money." She stood. "I think it best you remember that." She turned and marched from the house.

"We'll be in touch with more questions, I'm sure, ma'am." Maverick shot her a grin, then followed Blair to the truck.

"Something is rotten in Misty Hollow, Maverick."

He couldn't agree more.

Chapter Eleven

The FBI agents were late. While she waited, Blair nursed a bottle of water and thought over the questioning her and Maverick had done that day. They'd uncovered nothing more than a lot of uneasy feelings, gut reactions, all of which she had learned to take seriously. But would the FBI?

She glanced at Maverick sitting next to her. At least he believed her. At first, she'd wondered whether they could work effectively together with his surliness, but that had disappeared over time. He no longer seemed to have a chip on his shoulder because of his scars.

Her gaze drifted to the ridge of scar tissue that rose above his collar and up his neck. Someday, she'd like to hear more about how he got them.

The arrival of two agents pulled her attention back to where it belonged. Sheriff Westbrook introduced them as Special Agents Snowe and Larson.

"We're getting tired of coming to Misty Hollow, Sheriff." Agent Snowe glared. "You might want to work on getting control of your town."

The sheriff's face darkened. "We're secluded in a mountain valley. This location is prime for crime that doesn't want to be readily disposed of."

"At least Miss Oakley managed to save the girls." Agent Larson took a seat at the head of the table.

"With the help of Maverick," Blair said, crossing her arms.

"Who is?" Agent Larson tilted his head.

"I've deputized him." Sheriff Westbrook took a deep breath. "I thought it safer for Miss Oakley to have someone with her at all times. Especially now that we have a death on our hands."

"A suicide." Snowe rifled through the file on the table.

"Convenient," Blair mumbled.

"Excuse me?" The agent jerked to face her.

"I said, it's too convenient. Our prime witness turns up dead less than an hour after giving us vital information? The boy was murdered."

"We have no proof of that."

"It's a gut feeling."

A cold smile graced the agent's face. "We don't work on feelings, Miss Oakley."

"She hasn't been wrong yet." Maverick glared. "Blair and Diamond were vital to finding those girls."

They wouldn't have without Jacob, but his taking up for her still warmed Blair.

"Hmm." Agent Larson opened the file in front of him. "The two of you have questioned the parents recently?"

"Today." Blair folded her hands on top of the table. "Both sets of parents seem suspicious. Brittney Pitts acts afraid of her father. The Beanes weren't concerned in the least about the disappearance of their daughter." She turned to the sheriff. "Did they ever come for her?"

He shook his head. "I had a deputy drive her home. Against my better judgment, but we had no reason to keep her."

"The parents know something," Blair added.

"Another feeling?" Agent Snowe sneered.

"Yes." She hitched her chin in defiance.

Maverick nudged her with his knee and gave her a reassuring smile. "We'd like to focus more on the parents and a Vince Matterson."

"High school quarterback?" Snowe asked. "We'll question him."

"Are you taking over here?" Blair frowned.

"Unless another girl turns up missing, yes. At this time, you are free to return home."

Not a chance. Blair intended to see this through to the end. "I think I'll stick around for a while."

"Anyone questioned the teachers at the high school?" Larson asked, turning pages in the file.

"No." Westbrook shook his head. "Why don't we have Blair and Maverick concentrate on that so the two of you are free to find out whether Jacob Warren really committed suicide."

Snowe's eyes narrowed. "You telling us how to do our job, sheriff? Don't forget that you called for our help."

"When we still had a missing girl. Took you long enough to get here."

"We'd be glad to question the teachers," Blair said, hoping to diffuse the rising tension. "Since I plan on staying, I might as well be useful."

"Hmm." Larson turned his attention back to her. "You do have a commendable record. Yes, we've pulled your files. Yours, too, Maverick. You're somewhat of a hero from what we've read."

Blair widened her eyes at the quick change in the agent's attitude.

"Saved a family from a fire at risk of your own life. Well done. We could use someone like you in the agency."

"No, thanks. I'm happy at the ranch." Maverick narrowed his eyes. "And content to be used in whatever way the sheriff sees fit."

"Yes, it isn't the first time the sheriff has deputized the hands of Rocking W Ranch." Larson shrugged. "All ex-military, some ex-military police or special forces."

"True." Maverick grinned, the humor not reaching his eyes.

The tension in the room seemed to make Diamond nervous. Blair put a reassuring hand on her dog's head. "We'll start questioning the teachers first thing tomorrow."

"Good." Snowe nodded. "Larson and I will pay a visit to each set of parents. See whether we get the same 'feeling' you did." The agent chuckled.

"Are we finished here?" Blair didn't want to spend another minute with their condescending attitudes. Her stomach rumbled reminding her how long it had been since she'd eaten. "The day is growing late."

"Somewhere to be, ma'am?" Larson's grin widened.

"Yes. Supper."

~

Maverick declined the sheriff's invitation to stick around while he ordered in from the diner. "The three of you can hash this out. I'm taking Blair to the diner." He stood and offered her his hand.

"Same time, here tomorrow." Larson closed the file while Snowe flipped over the case board to its blank side. "We'll compare notes then."

Great. Another unpleasant evening to look forward to.

"I do not like those agents." Blair yanked open the passenger door to the truck.

"Neither do I." He grinned. "Don't let them bother you. They'll figure out soon enough that your feelings are valid. I did."

"Thank you." She gave a sweet smile and climbed into the truck.

At the diner, they were led to a table near the window so they could keep an eye on where Diamond's leash was attached to a post out front. Maverick glanced at the special. Meatloaf. No thanks. A burger, fully loaded, sounded better.

Blair ordered soup and a salad. "I know it might sound ridiculous, but I really do think the Pitts and Beanes know something."

"I agree. At least with the Beanes." Speaking of the two, they entered the diner looking squeaky clean, although a bit wobbly, wearing clothes that still bore the fold marks. "Somebody seems to have gone shopping."

"Makes you wonder where they suddenly got the money, because if I'm not mistaken, they drove up in a brand-new truck." She motioned out the window.

"Very curious." He grinned. "We'll have some interesting questions to ask next time we talk to them."

"If the agents don't have them running scared. Doesn't it seem strange that they wouldn't have Lesley with them after she just returned home? I wouldn't let my child out of my sight until those responsible were behind bars."

"Maybe that's what Pitts is doing."

"Maybe, but something still seems off there, too." She sat back as their food was brought to them.

"I've got a burger for the dog." The server smiled. "Is it okay if I take it to her?"

"Absolutely." Blair smiled. "Thank you."

"Anything for the dog that found my friend."

"Which one?"

"Lesley. We've been best friends since first grade."

Maverick glanced at her name tag. Lilly. "What can you tell us about her family life, Lilly?"

The girl glanced to where the Beanes sat. "They pretty much ignore her. The two spend more time at the bar than they do at home. They don't abuse her or anything, they just…" she shrugged. "I shouldn't say anything. I need to get back to work. Give me a wave if you need anything." She rushed away from the table.

"Confirmation things aren't rosy at the Beane home." Blair forked a mouthful of salad. "Doesn't mean they know anything about their daughter's disappearance, but if I were to bet, I'd say they did. I really want to know where they got money all of a sudden."

Maverick didn't want to contemplate. The idea that popped into his head, that they may have sold their daughter, was too awful to think about. "Mind driving by the Beane place after we eat? I want to make sure Lesley is okay."

If the Beanes had sold their daughter, wouldn't they have had to give the money back now that Lesley was home? Or were they working for the one in charge in another capacity? He suddenly had more questions than he did answers.

Questions that needed to be handed over to the agents. But, first, he wanted an answer or two.

They ate quickly, paid the bill, added a tip, and drove out to the Beane place. Maverick wanted a chance to speak to Lesley before her parents showed up, and he counted on them heading to the local bar after they ate.

A single light shined in a front window of the Beane house. Leaving the dog in the truck, Maverick and Blair stepped onto the porch. Maverick knocked.

A few seconds later, Lesley peered between the curtains, then opened the door. "Hello?"

Maverick smiled. "We're just checking up on you. Everything okay?"

She nodded and joined them on the porch. "I'm sticking close to home for a while, because, well, you know."

"Yes, we do." Blair laid a hand on her shoulder. "Do you need anything? Are you afraid to be here alone? We saw your parents at the diner in new clothes with a new truck."

She shrugged. "Dad said he got a raise. They bought me a new pair of jeans. Yes, I'm fine. I'm used to being here alone. I get the TV all to myself."

"Have you returned to school?" Blair asked.

"Not yet. Monday, maybe. My friend Lilly brought me my schoolwork, so I don't get behind." Tears welled in her eyes. "I don't want people looking at me funny."

"I can understand that." Maverick peered around her to the inside of the house. Cluttered, dirty, with furniture that had seen better days. "I'd like to give you my phone number, Lesley. In case you need anything or get scared. Do you have a cell phone?"

"Hold on. My parents don't know I have one. I bought it with tutoring money. I help tutor the football players." She ducked into the house.

"Same as Brittney." Blair's wide-eyed gaze followed the girl.

"Yep."

When Lesley brought out the phone, he entered his phone number into her contacts. "I'm serious. Anytime you need something or get scared, you call me. Got it?"

She nodded. "Thanks. It's nice to have someone I can call if I need to."

That someone should be her parents, but since it wasn't, he was more than happy to fill the void. "Lock the door behind you. Don't open it to anyone but us, your parents, or the police. Not even kids from school."

The girl paled. "You think someone from school wants to hurt me?"

"I didn't say that. We only want you to be very careful. Okay?" He wanted her a bit frightened, a little paranoid. It might be the only way to keep her safe.

Chapter Twelve

A knock on the door pulled Blair from her slumber. She glanced at the clock and groaned. Not even daylight.

When the knocking persisted and Diamond growled low in her throat, Blair sat up and tossed aside the sheet she'd covered up with. "This better be important."

Realizing that it very well could be, she bounded from bed and down the stairs to open the door. Maverick stood there holding a thermos and basket. "What's wrong?"

"Nothing." He grinned. "I thought you could use a break before we head to the school. Get dressed. I've got coffee and sausage biscuits. There's something I want to show you."

"Come in. Give me five minutes." She thundered back up the stairs and grabbed some clothes from the dresser. In less than five minutes, anticipation coursing through her, she rejoined him. "This better be good."

"It will be. I promise."

He drove them to the top of the mountain, then led her to a rock overhang. He spread a tattered old army blanket he'd pulled from behind the seat of his truck and motioned for her to sit before pouring them both cups of steaming coffee. "It won't be long."

When the sun started its ascent, Maverick took Blair's hand and pulled her to her feet. A bolt of electricity shot up her arm.

What was wrong with her? This wasn't the first time he'd touched her, but it was the first time she'd reacted this way. She glanced at him.

"Don't look at me. Look over the valley. There. See?" He pointed.

"Oh, wow."

The sun kissed a mist that hung over the valley so thick she felt as if she could take a step off the ledge and walk across. Hints of rose kissed the silver mist. "So, this is how the town got its name."

"Yep." He gave her a hand a squeeze. "My favorite place in the world."

She glanced at the log house behind them. "Won't they care that we're here?"

"No. Folks come here all the time." His warm gaze landed on hers mirroring the feelings rushing through her.

Longing, desire, and a hint of something much deeper. Something that had been growing between them that she'd wanted to squelch, to ignore. Maybe she could imagine something more between them now that they weren't searching for a missing girl.

Without speaking, Maverick leaned in, his lips brushing against hers with a tenderness that brought tears to her eyes. She closed her eyes and leaned in. The world around them faded until only the two of them remained.

When they finally pulled apart, Blair felt even more convinced that she could float across the mist over the valley. Her heart pounded as Maverick traced a finger down her cheek.

"The mist is disappearing," he said softly.

"What? Oh." She pulled herself from her trance and watched as the mist dissipated. When the town of Misty Hollow showed below, she smiled.

"I've wanted to do that for a few days." With his forefinger, he tilted her face to his. "I hope that was okay."

More than okay, actually. Magical. Maybe the magic came from the view, but his kiss had only added to the atmosphere. "I don't mind at all." Her face heated, and she ducked her head.

"Hungry?"

She nodded and returned to the blanket as a light flickered on in the house behind them. No one came out to order them to leave. No one came onto the porch to see what they did. Envy for those who lived in such a wonderful place filtered through her.

"Are there other views of the mist like this one?" She opened the basket and handed him a sandwich before taking one for herself.

"I'm sure there is, but this is the easiest to get to."

"I'd like to live in a place like this someday. I'd wake up to watch the mist every morning no matter how hot or cold the day." She bit into her breakfast. Flaky buttery-ness mingled with the bite of sausage. Mrs. White could definitely cook.

"You've gone silent. Are you sure my kissing you wasn't out of line?" Concern flickered in Maverick's eyes.

"I'm sure." She smiled and got to her knees. "In fact, I'll show you how not out of line the kiss was." She leaned forward and kissed him.

His arms wrapped around her, pulling her onto his lap as he deepened the kiss. "Stay a while, Blair."

"What will I do if I'm not working?" She stared into his eyes.

"Get to know me. Unless you can't..." He waved a hand in front of his face.

"That doesn't bother me, Maverick. Take off your shirt. I want to see you."

Shock registered in his eyes. He opened his mouth, then closed it before slowing unbuttoning the pearl buttons on his plaid shirt. "Don't say I didn't warn you."

She kept smiling. "Your scars will not repulse me, Maverick."

"We'll see." His voice shook as he shrugged off the shirt.

She ran her hands over the ridges of scar tissue. He was still the most beautiful man she'd ever seen. She pressed her lips to the scar that rose from his shoulder and up his neck.

He took a sharp breath. "Are you trying to kill me?"

She laughed and sat back. "Just showing you how non-repulsive you are." She traced his scars with her fingers, sending his skin quivering.

~

Maverick had never felt more vulnerable or exposed. He relaxed a bit to see that the occupants of the house didn't step outside. Still, he didn't want to put on a show. He quickly put his shirt back on.

"Pity." Blair gave a flirtatious grin. "I like looking at you."

"Since it would be improper to do the same to you, we'd better cool down." He chuckled. Who was this amazing woman who could see his scars and still smile? Could it really be that his scars bothered him more than others? Did most people see past his disfigurement to the real Maverick?

"Tell me what happened," Blair said softly. "I really do want to know."

He locked gazes with her for a moment before nodding. "I was a volunteer fire fighter in a small town outside Fayetteville. The blaze had grown too big for us to fight." Memories assaulted him, turning his blood cold.

"The man of the house came running up shouting about his wife and child. No one had seen anyone come out of the house. The fire chief said the fire was too big for any of us to go inside."

"But you did."

"Yes." He closed his eyes and took a deep breath. "I entered through the mud room which didn't burn as hot. I found the woman and toddler passed out from smoke inhalation in the hall. They'd tried to get out. I slung the woman over my shoulder and picked up the child. Before I had gone more than ten feet, the ceiling groaned. I threw them toward the open door right before a burning beam fell on me. I wasn't strong enough to get it off.

"I woke up in the hospital to everyone calling me a hero. Said I saved the woman and her child, but almost died myself."

"You are a hero." She cupped his cheek.

He leaned into her touch. "I like to think I did what anyone would do."

"But they didn't, Maverick. You did. Everyone else was too afraid."

"I was pretty afraid when I woke up in the hospital covered in bandages, in fierce pain. It took several months of healing and physical therapy before I could function."

"You're a very strong person." She sat back. "The world is better because you're in it."

Uncomfortable with the turn of the conversation, he got to his feet. "Ready? We've got a lot of work to do."

Confusion clouded her eyes. "Okay." She put their garbage in the basket and stood. "I'd like to run back to my cottage to grab my notepad, if that's okay."

They made the drive back to the ranch in silence. Maverick hated reverting back to his quiet self, but reliving the nightmare had been a lot. He wanted to forget that day, but he got a reminder every time he looked in the mirror.

He parked in front of the main house and followed Blair around the back to her cottage. A white sheet of paper waved from her door.

Blair's hand trembled as she removed the note. "Leave town. Take your dog. Bad things will happen if you keep asking questions."

Maverick glanced at the camera in the corner of the porch. "Let's go take a look at the security feed. We might recognize whoever left the note. Then, we call the sheriff."

"Okay." She held the note between two fingers. "My prints are on this paper. Stupid rookie mistake."

"Maybe the person who left it left prints, too." He led her to Wyatt's office. After explaining the need to look at the cameras, his boss nodded.

"Let's take a look." Dylan pulled up the feed. "They're wearing a hoodie and it's still dark outside."

"The time stamp shows the note was left just minutes after we left." His heart skipped a beat. Had they known Blair wasn't home or had they thought she'd see the note when she left for the day? Either way, they'd been too close. "That could be any male in town."

"About five ten, Caucasian, not bowed in the shoulders," Blair said. "We're looking for someone young. Forties or less."

"Fits a lot of folks in this town," Dylan said. "I'll save this and send it to the sheriff."

"That should be okay until we meet this afternoon." Blair straightened. "This isn't the first time I've received a threat during my line of work. It won't stop me from doing what needs to be done. If I'd been home, Diamond would've alerted me to the culprit. I might have caught them in the act."

"And been harmed in the process." Maverick frowned. Was she regretting their morning outing? Had he read more into the time and the kiss than the situation warranted? He hoped not. He felt as if he and Blair had turned a serious corner in their relationship. If there was a relationship. Maybe it was all in his head, and she'd simply been caught up in the moment. It might not have meant anything to her at all.

"Let's head to the high school. The sooner we figure out the people responsible, the sooner—"

"You can go home." Maverick spun and marched

from the office.

Blair caught up with him on the porch. "Did I say something wrong?"

"No."

"Then why the attitude?" She grabbed his arm and turned him to face her. "We had a nice morning, Maverick. Why are you trying to spoil things?"

"I'm not." He pulled free.

"Yes, you are." She crossed her arms and glared up at him. "Tell me what's wrong."

"What if you'd been home?"

"Then I might have caught this person in the act."

"And been harmed!"

"So, you say. Diamond wouldn't let anyone get close enough to harm me."

"Even Diamond can't take down someone if they're armed."

"We don't know they were armed." She hitched her chin. "Don't worry about me. I can take care of myself."

He took a step back. Take care of herself? Where did that leave him? He wanted to be the one who took care of her. The thought surprised him. Ever since the fire, he'd try to stay inside his safe little bubble.

Then, along came Blair Oakley and her dog and everything changed.

Chapter Thirteen

He narrowed his eyes as the truck with the cowboy and the woman parked in the high school parking lot. How many times did they need to come and disrupt his day? He was a busy man!

If people did their jobs, this would all be over with, and his bank account would be a whole lot fatter. He kicked the metal desk next to him and turned away from the window.

He'd thought using good-looking boys would work to his benefit. Nope. He should've used the tried-and-true method of snatch-and-grab a girl from the street and move her fast.

Not only was the cowboy and the woman a nuisance, but that sheriff seemed to be everywhere, him and his deputies. Now, the FBI had been called in. Things were getting very messy.

A glance at the clock sent him from his classroom. With his prep time almost over, he needed to grab a bite to eat. The arriving meddlers were bound to want to talk to him at some point, and he had some workers to warn not to say too much or they'd end up like Jacob.

Something he regretted. Willing workers were few in Misty Hollow.

~

"I'm starting to feel as if I need to get my own desk at this school." Blair started to open the front door, only to have Maverick beat her to it.

"This will all be over soon." He followed her to the front desk where the administrative assistant smiled and motioned them to the conference room.

"I'll let Mr. White know you're here." The unspoken "again" hung in the air.

Blair felt like the hamster running on a wheel and getting nowhere. Thankfully, they'd rescued Brittney and Lesley, but the person responsible still walked free. That, alone, made her feel like a failure.

Diamond, always tuned into Blair's emotions, nudged her hand. Blair patted the dog and smiled as she entered the conference room and took a seat ready for another long few hours of questions with few answers.

Maverick shot her a questioning look. She widened her smile, hoping it looked reassuring, and opened the notepad she set in front of her.

"Good morning." Mr. White entered the room. "The students again?"

"Every teacher of the victims and the football players, please." Blair's face started to ache from her false smile. "Just some last minute follow up questions."

"I'll get you a list and have them start filing in." He backed from the room, closing the door behind him.

The high school English teacher arrived first. An middle-aged woman in a flowered dress and brown sweater sat across from them. "What can I help you with?"

Blair glanced at the list the administrative assistant had handed her. "Ms. Roberts?"

"Yes."

"What can you tell me about Vince Matterson?"

She blinked in confusion, then straightened her shoulders. "Good grades, cocky attitude, thinks he runs the school."

"How does he act toward the girls, Brittney Pitts and Lesley Beane in particular?"

"Brittney tutors him, I believe. I haven't seen him associate with Lesley, but she's a quiet girl who stays to herself, does her work, and doesn't cause any problems. That girl could be a writer someday, if I do say so myself."

"What about the crowd he runs around with?" Blair's pen poised above the notepad.

"Same. That group is all made from the same mold. I do believe Lesley tutors one of them, but I'm not sure."

"Any of the teachers seem overly familiar with any of the mentioned students?"

She frowned. "The coach is close with his players, but that's normal. The rest of us teachers are available for teaching and being a confidante when needed, but nothing inappropriate, I assure you. Our principal, Mr. Armstrong, he's on vacation, lucky man, wouldn't allow it." She took a deep breath through her nose. "I must admit to feeling sorry for poor Mr. White. He had no idea what he would have to deal with when he stepped into Mr. Armstrong's shoes for a few weeks. Who knew all this horrible nonsense would happen."

Blair sighed. "Thank you for your time, Ms.

Roberts."

The history and math teacher had nothing more to add than she did. Blair tossed down her pen. "This is a waste of time."

"Don't give up yet." Maverick bumped her with his shoulder. "We still have a few to question. Somebody here knows something. You keep asking the questions, and I'll keep watching for signs of lying. Someone here knows something. We'll find out what that something is."

"Hmm." She nodded and glanced up as a big man with a paunch entered the room. His school tee-shirt stretched over a gut that hung over his knee length shorts. The coach. Her fake smile trembled under his cold stare.

"Make this quick. I've got football practice in an hour."

Blair sat back and crossed her arms. "Tell me about your players. Vince in particular."

He narrowed his eyes. "All on the straight and narrow. I won't have it any other way. If they do wrong, they sit the bench. Third time, they're off the team. These boys see sports as their way out of this town. They do what I tell them."

Would that include kidnapping fellow students? "What do you know about Brittney Pitts?"

"Don't know the girl well, but her father and I have a beer at the bar together once in a while."

"Lesley Beane?"

"I don't hang out with drunkards, and her parents are both drunkards."

"They seem to be doing well for themselves lately."

"Not any of my business. Maybe the lazy Beane found a real job."

"What kind of work does he do?"

"Whatever puts liquor money in his pocket."

She folded her hands on the table and leaned forward. "You don't like him."

He shrugged. "Like I said, I don't really know the guy."

"You have a strong opinion about him for not knowing him."

"I've got eyes, don't I?"

"Tell me more about your friendship with Mr. Pitts."

"I don't see how that is any of your business. You're search and rescue, if I'm not mistaken."

"The sheriff has asked for our help," Maverick interrupted. "We can let him know you were unwilling to talk to us. Maybe you'd be more comfortable at the sheriff's office with him or the FBI questioning you."

His brow furrowed. "Am I a suspect?"

"That remains to be determined." Blair tilted to her head. "Tell us about your friendship with Mr. Pitts."

~

Something didn't ring true about the coach. Maverick kept his gaze focused on the man. He didn't squirm, but his face had darkened with each question. The man didn't sit as relaxed as the teachers before him. Tension kept his back against the chair, hands clenched tight enough to turn his knuckles white.

"Like I said, we have a beer together once or twice a week. We both have stressful jobs. It's a good way to unwind."

"Coaching is stressful?" Blair arched a brow.

"Of course, it is. I'm dealing with kids."

"Hmm." Her lips curled into a smile. "The ones I've met have been wonderful. Well, except for Vince. He's a bit of a trial, isn't he?"

"Can be, but he's a good boy deep down."

"How deep down, Mr. Lawrence? So deep that abducting a young girl would come easy for him?"

"Preposterous."

"What about Jacob Warren?"

"Tragedy."

Maverick mimicked the man's body language. "Authorities seem to think he committed suicide. Any reason?"

"No. The boy seemed the happy sort until lately. Then something seemed to be bothering him. Maybe he got into drugs."

"Was he the type?" Maverick slipped into the role of questioning, leaving Blair to take notes. "Nobody else seems to think so."

"Kids are complicated creatures. Who knows what goes on inside their heads."

"I would think their football coach would have an idea. After all, they spend a lot of time together, right?"

"What are you saying?" If his face got any redder, the man might pop something.

"What if he didn't kill himself, coach?" Maverick leaned back. "What if the boy knew too much, maybe had a guilty conscience and wanted to tell what he knew? Who would want him out of the picture?"

"I have no idea what you're talking about. If you want to ask something, stop beating around the bush."

"Okay. Did you kill Jacob Warren or know who did?"

"No."

"Do you know who abducted Brittney Pitts or Lesley Beane?"

"No."

"If we were to question Mr. Pitts, would he give us the same answer?"

"How the hell would I know?" The man lunged to his feet. "Like I said, I've got football practice to get to. You know where I am if you have any more ridiculous accusations."

"We aren't accusing anyone, Mr. Lawrence. We're simply trying to find answers to the abduction of two innocent girls."

"At least they're both back home where they belong." He whirled and marched from the room.

"He's lying." Maverick stood. "Maybe the FBI agents can get more out of him."

"I got the same feeling." She closed her notepad and slipped it into her bag. "I think we should pay another visit to Mr. Pitts. See if he's got looser lips than his friend."

Before heading to the sheriff's office, they stopped at the bank and asked to see Mr. Pitts. The receptionist frowned but left her desk and went to inquire if he had the time.

"What if he doesn't want to talk to us?" Blair asked.

"Then, we'll let the agents handle him. I'm sure he'll talk to us. We're less intimidating." Maverick grinned.

"Me, maybe. You're scary." She laughed.

"I'm a big teddy bear." He put his hand on the small of her back as the receptionist waved him to follow her.

Mr. Pitts sat behind a large mahogany desk, a scowl on his face as he hung up his phone. "I don't have a lot of time. What can I do for you?"

"Was that Coach Lawrence on the phone?" Maverick asked.

"A customer, not that it's any of your business."

"We've been hearing a lot of that today." Maverick took a seat without being asked. Blair did the same.

The banker glared at Diamond. "I don't like animals in my bank."

"Service dog." Maverick grinned. "You can't keep her out."

"What do you want?"

"How's your daughter?"

"Fine. Didn't you see her in the waiting area?"

"Nope."

Pitts jumped to his feet and rushed toward the door.

"Maybe she's in the restroom." Blair moved from the door. "Would you like me to check?"

"I'll have my receptionist check."

"Afraid I'll ask her some questions?" Blair grinned. "Like maybe why she feels like a prisoner around you?"

He stiffened and turned to face her. "What does that mean?"

"You don't like her out of your sight. She hasn't returned to school, walks with her head down, all of which, from what I can gather, is not typical behavior for her."

You go, girl. Maverick grinned, enjoying the

show. He almost felt sorry for the man. Almost.

"I'm concerned about what my daughter has been through as any good father would." He returned to his desk and barked an order into his phone for the receptionist to locate Brittney and send her to his office. "I assure you," he said, returning his attention back to Blair and Maverick, "that I am not keeping my daughter prisoner."

"Then why are you so alarmed that she isn't sitting where you left her?" Maverick kept a sharp gaze on the man. "You feeling okay, sir? You're looking a little pale."

"I think I'm coming down with a stomach bug." He took a deep breath, releasing it slowly as he resumed his seat. "Are we finished here?"

"The coach said the two of you go to the bar a couple of times a week. Ever see the Beanes there?"

"They're always there."

"You and the coach close?"

"Pretty much. We've known each other for about three years." He pulled a pencil from a coffee mug he used as a pencil holder and tapped it on his desk blotter. "Me and the missus would have lunch with him and his wife before she died of cancer a couple of years ago. Why the interest in our friendship?"

"Because, Mr. Pitts, I think the two of you are involved in what is happening in Misty Hollow." Maverick leaned forward, his hands dangling between his knees. "I also believe that one or both of you know more about the death of Jacob Warren than either of you are letting on."

The man paled further. "I think it's time for the two of you to leave."

Maverick stood and headed for the door. He opened it for Blair, then turned back. "As the authorities say, don't leave town, Mr. Pitts." He grinned and stepped from the room, leaving the door open.

Chapter Fourteen

Blair woke to the smell of smoke.

Diamond's barks from the bottom floor echoed through the cottage.

Tossing aside the blankets, Blair bounded from bed and downstairs. Flames licked at the window over the kitchen sink. Fire? Fire!

She grabbed her bag with notes and tossed it out the window before grabbing clothes and other items. She tucked her laptop under her arm and slipped shoes on her feet before dashing outside with the laptop. As she set it in the grass, the cowbell from the main house clanged.

She whirled and dashed back into the cottage to retrieve as many of her few possessions as she could before she succumbed to smoke. She coughed and pulled the neckline of her tee-shirt over her mouth and nose. "Outside, Diamond!" The dog barked and Blair repeated the order.

Frantic, she studied the small house for anything she might have forgotten.

"Blair!" Maverick grabbed her from behind.

"Wait. I need to make sure I have everything."

She tried pulling free.

"Please." His voice broke before he slung her over his shoulder and bolted from the burning building.

Outside, he set her on her feet a safe distance from the fire. The glow lit up the early morning. "You know how fire scares me. What were you thinking just standing there?"

"I can't forget anything." She glared up at him. "I was fine. The fire hadn't spread much."

"Well, it has now." He jerked his chin toward the inferno before pulling her into a hug. "I don't know what I would've done if you'd been lying on the floor unconscious."

"Exactly what you did do," she mumbled against his chest. "Come in and rescue me." She lifted her head to face him. "You didn't think twice, did you? You ran into that fire after me."

"No, I didn't think twice." His hold tightened. "I can't lose you, Blair."

She cupped his face. "I'm not going anywhere."

The other ranch hands, including the boss, buckets and wet blankets in hand raced toward the cottage. Before the first water hit the flames, the roof collapsed with a groan.

Blair yelped and leaped back as the heat seared her skin. She'd thought the meeting with the agents and the sheriff the night before had been bad. The agents had scoffed at her thoughts that the coach and banker were involved. Told her she jumped to conclusions, and she be more careful before accusing townspeople.

Maverick had to back her up, to no avail. They'd left and she'd tossed and turned before falling into a fitful sleep, then a sleep so deep she hadn't seen or heard anyone around the cottage. "The camera?"

"Maybe." Maverick's arm moved to her shoulder, and he tucked her tight against him. "Since the fire was set at the back of the cottage, I doubt we'll see anything."

"We can try." She slipped free of his hold and retrieved her laptop before it got trampled.

"Yes, we can try."

"I don't think this is part of your things." Dylan handed her a sheet of paper.

Blair snatched it. "I warned you. Leave now or things get real ugly." She sighed and folded the warning, then shoved it into her bag. "I'm sorry about the cottage."

"The cottage can be rebuilt, Blair," he said. "The important thing is that no one was hurt. You can move into the main house."

It might be best for everyone if she moved back to the motel. Someone other than herself could have been badly injured. She glanced at Maverick. She didn't want to be far from him. His presence made her feel safe even with danger stalking her.

She coughed again, then cleared her throat before starting the process of picking up the things she tossed out the door. Sirens wailed, then cut off as emergency vehicles pulled close.

"Let's get you checked out by a medic." Maverick handed her a few items. "The hands can take these to an empty room in the house."

"I'm fine."

"For me. Please." The earnestness in his voice gave her pause.

She nodded. "Okay." Despite his intense fear of

fire, he'd come to her rescue. The least she could do is grant him the simple request of getting checked out.

After a few minutes of wearing an oxygen mask, the medic proclaimed her good. "You should get changed, though, and rid yourself of the smoke odor."

"I will, thanks." She hopped from the back of the ambulance and stood next to Maverick to watch as the fire department sprayed hoses of water on the embers of the burned cottage. "I liked that little place."

"There's another that's vacant, but I think the boss is right. You should move into the house where it's safer."

"The big house can be set on fire all the same." Tears blurred her vision, and she sniffed.

He jerked his attention from the fire to her. "Are you sure you're okay?"

"Yes." She nodded. "This is bad, Maverick. Someone really doesn't want me here."

"That's because we're getting very close to finding out who is responsible for these abductions. Finding those girls took a lot of money out of someone's pocket."

"Good." She smiled through her tears. She intended to mess up the someone's life a whole lot more.

~

Lilly McClintock's car sputtered and died halfway between the diner and her friend Lesley's house. "Not now." She leaned her head against the steering wheel for a minute before opening her door and climbing out. The last thing she needed was for her car to break down.

She popped the hood and stared at the engine. Not

that she had the faintest idea what to look for. With a sigh, she leaned through the driver's side and turned on her flashers. Eventually, someone would stop to help her.

Darkness hadn't yet fled from the sun's rising. The road, cast in shadow, looked menacing. Fear rose in her throat. She crossed her arms and leaned against the dead car. When headlights appeared over the hill, she pushed away from the vehicle and went to stand off the shoulder.

A battered truck stopped. "Need help?"

She squinted and peered into the cab. Recognizing the driver, she nodded. "Yes, thank you. I don't have cell service here. Can I use yours to call a tow truck?"

"Sure but let me take a look first. It might be something simple." He smiled and exited his truck.

"Thanks. I appreciate it." She stood next to him as he bent over the engine.

"It's your battery, I think." He straightened and pulled something from his pocket.

The syringe glittered in the moonlight.

"You." She staggered back.

He lunged forward, plunging the needle into her neck.

Everything went black as she fell into his arms.

~

When Maverick saw the flames eating the cottage Blair stayed in, his heart had stopped. He'd only hesitated a moment before rushing to her aid. Now that the adrenaline had stopped burning through his veins, he sagged into a dining room chair.

Blair had taken the medic's advice and gone to shower and change.

He covered his face with trembling hands. Nausea rolled in his stomach. He should seek help for his fear of fire. Things would've had a very different outcome if he'd succumbed to that fear. Blair might not be alive. He wouldn't have been able to live with himself.

Mrs. White set a cup of coffee in front of him. "A hero again."

"Hardly."

"You very well might have saved that girl's life." She set a bowl of water in front of Diamond. "Despite the way you're trembling, you did what had to be done. That makes you a hero."

He made a sound in his throat and reached for his cup of coffee. He'd placed a call to the sheriff the moment Blair went upstairs. The man promised to come out as soon as possible. That had been fifteen minutes ago.

"That's better." Blair entered the kitchen and accepted a cup of coffee from Mrs. White. "I smell better, too." She sniffed. "You should shower, Maverick. The smell isn't as strong on you, but it's there."

"I will." He forced a smile, then tugged on a strand of her wet hair. "Did you manage to get everything you needed from the cottage?"

"I think so. My laptop and the case notes were the most important, and they were the first I grabbed." She took a seat across from him. "Thank you again."

"You were almost ready to come out."

She sighed. "But I wasn't out. My stubbornness could have gotten me killed."

He laughed. "Yep." His laugh sounded forced. "We need a better plan at finding this person before someone does end up dead." Other than poor Jacob Warren who he believed had been killed for letting him and Blair know where the girls were held.

"I agree, but I don't have a clue where to start other than digging more into Lawrence and Pitts. Maybe we should pay a visit to the bar where they hang out? Bartenders usually know a lot about their regulars." She added cream and sugar to her coffee, the spoon clanking the sides of the cup as she stirred. "I really do think they're involved in this somehow."

"I agree. We'll go by there tonight." He stared into his half empty cup. "Weren't you scared, Blair?"

"Of course, I was, but I couldn't let my things burn."

"Excuse me?" The fire chief stood at the back door. "Got a minute?"

"Sure," Maverick said. "Come on in."

The man entered. "It'll warrant further investigation, but it appears an accelerant was used."

Maverick had figured as much.

"Wyatt said he wasn't able to see anyone on the security camera. They must have entered from the woods. The cameras out there were destroyed."

Maverick nodded. "Figures." They weren't any closer to catching those responsible. "Keep us informed."

"Will do." The fire chief left as the sheriff entered.

"A regular revolving door," Maverick muttered getting to his feet. His heart skipped a beat at the look on the sheriff's face. "What is it?"

"Lilly McClintock is missing. Her disabled vehicle was found on Highway 64. No sign of her and the keys are still in the ignition?"

"The server from the diner?" Blair asked.

"Yes." The sheriff removed his hat. "No signs of a struggle, but a syringe was found next to her car. We've got an APB out on her, but well…"

The abductor had struck again. Maverick's shoulders slumped. "We'll set out to try tracking her from her last known location." Not that he expected them to find anything.

He also didn't think they'd get as lucky at finding her as they were Brittney and Lesley. Whoever took her would be more careful this time. Except…why leave the syringe behind unless it, too, was a warning?

Chapter Fifteen

Blair stood near Lilly's car while Diamond sniffed around the vehicle. When the dog glanced her way, she said, "Find."

Diamond let out one bark and turned in a circle. When Blair repeated the command, the dog repeated her circling.

"The trail goes nowhere. Lilly must have been transferred to another vehicle at this point." Blair's shoulders slumped. Car broke down, someone stops to help, knocks her out, then shoves her into whatever they were driving. "She could be anywhere."

"We're out here, we might as well try." Maverick shrugged.

"You're no more hopeful than I am." She eyed the yellow marker the crime scene techs had placed where they'd found the syringe.

Tire tracks faded onto the asphalt. Maybe someone would be able to get a make and model on the vehicle. She pulled out her cell phone and took photos, even though she knew the sheriff's department had already taken them. Maybe she'd find something they missed, a clue to lead them straight to Lilly. Could she and Maverick get lucky a third time by saving Lilly?

No, she didn't believe in luck. What they needed to do was find someone willing to talk as Jacob had.

"Let's head down the road, back toward town. Maybe we'll see something," Maverick suggested.

"You don't think they'll use a cabin on the mountain again?" Blair motioned for Diamond to come.

"No, I think they'll hide her right under our noses. They've already tried the out-in-the-middle-of nowhere approach."

"The local motel?"

"Possibly. It's worth a look." He slid into the driver's seat. "If not there, then we'll search every available empty house and building in town." He gave her hand a squeeze. "We'll find her. We won't lose Lilly."

Blair nodded, holding onto his promise with both hands. "What if she isn't held in an empty building? What if she's at the coach's or the Pitts'? If they are involved, it's quite possible—"

"Do you think Brittney would know? It can't be too difficult to get her phone number."

"I don't think she's involved other than being a victim herself." Blair frowned.

"That's not what I'm saying. What I'm suggesting is that, since her father keeps her close to his side, she might have heard something. It won't hurt to try if the motel is a bust."

"Okay." At this point, she'd try anything.

As suspected, no one matching Lilly's description showed up at the motel. The manager promised to call if anyone, mostly a single man, rented a room. The young man knew Lilly from the diner and would keep an eye out for her. Having the girl show up there would be too easy, not to mention dangerous for the manager. No, whoever had her would want as few eyes on their deed as possible.

"Where to now?"

"Since Sheriff Westbrook has pretty much given us free rein in our investigating, let's drive to abandoned buildings I know about. If that doesn't pan out, we'll go with your idea of contacting Brittney. Call the coffee shop and see whether whoever is working there today will give you Brittney's number."

Blair dialed the coffee shop. "Hey, can you give me Brittney's phone number? This is her cousin, Blair, and I'm supposed to be at her house. I'm running late and I've lost her number."

"Sure." The girl who answered the phone rattled off a number. "I hope she's doing okay after…well, you know."

"That's why I'm here. Thanks!" Blair hung up.

"Smooth." Maverick grinned.

"Young girls like to believe the best. That's why they're such easy targets." Especially if they know the person out to harm them. Blair was even more convinced Vince Matterson was part of what was happening in Misty Hollow. "It's not only girls who are taken, boys, too, but mostly female teens and early twenties. Although, there have been some as young as nine or ten." She closed her eyes, trying to shut out the horrors she'd witnessed in her job.

"It's a rough world sometimes."

"It is." She dialed Brittney's phone, praying the girl would answer and not one of her parents. "Hey, Brittney. This is Blair Oakley. Act like it's one of your friends, okay?"

"Sure."

Good girl. "I hate to be the bearer of bad news, but Lilly from the diner has been taken. Would you have any idea where she might be held?"

"Yeah." Her chipper tone sounded forced.

"Are you alone?"

"Uh-huh. I'm busy doing my homework."

"Got it. Is there a way you can sneak out? Meet us at the picnic table by the lake, okay? The one by site number five. Half an hour." The last time she'd been there, Blair had noticed site five was rather secluded opposed to some of the others. Unless the place was busy, they should be able to talk to Brittney without interruption.

"Sure! Let me finish up here. Bye." The girl hung up.

Blair slipped her phone into her pocket. "Let's hope she manages to get away. She replied affirmative to my asking if she knew where Lilly was being held."

"That's good."

"Hopefully, her helping us doesn't end up the same way as Jacob's helping did."

"Don't be a pessimist. We're going to end this." He squeezed her hand again and turned the truck toward the lake. "These people will be behind bars soon."

She wished she shared his optimism. Usually, she did. What was different with this job? The fact that as soon as one girl was rescued, another was taken. The job seemed never-ending, something Blair wasn't used to.

When she added in how the idea of leaving Misty

Hollow left her empty, she wanted to crawl into a hole. Staying in Misty Hollow with Maverick depended on her having a job. A job that required someone, most likely a young person, to go missing. What kind of a sick person did that make her?

Unless...she could find a way to make her job work while using Misty Hollow as her base. But that depended on Maverick, didn't it? He hadn't tried to kiss her again. Instead, other than holding her hand, he'd remained distant. As if he regretted their tender moment up on the mountain.

Maybe he wouldn't want her to stay.

~

Brittney slipped out the back door of the bank on the pretense of using the women's room. Her father would figure out her deception soon enough. But he was in a meeting. If she was lucky, she'd be back from the bank with him not knowing a thing.

If he found out she'd snuck out again...she put a hand to her cheek. Makeup wouldn't cover the next bruise.

She darted down the alley and into the strip of woods that lined the highway. After looking both ways, she sprinted across the highway, then the railroad tracks, and to where the lake shimmered in the distance.

She could've flagged down a car, but after Jacob's death she didn't want to involve anyone. Tears burned her eyes. She'd wanted Jacob to ask her to the prom next year. Now, the two of them had no chance to see what dating each other would've been like. She'd die before going on a date with Vince.

Not that he hadn't tried. Thankfully, because of her father's plans for her, he'd made all the boys stay a safe distance away from Brittney now that she was back home. Plans! Like she'd do any of the plans he wanted to make for her.

No, she'd rather die than put a girl through what she'd gone through. Or worse.

~

"There she is." Maverick stood from the picnic table. "Only ten minutes late."

"Sorry." Brittney's chest heaved. "We have to make this fast. My father is in a meeting. If he finds me gone…"

"Got it." He helped her sit on the concrete bench. "Five minutes, then we'll give you a ride a block from the bank. You'll be fine."

She nodded. "I heard voices in the basement. My dad and someone else. They whispered. Then a girl's voice before they told her to shut up. I think Lilly might be in my basement."

"Your father is involved?" Blair's face darkened.

"Yes, but he isn't the boss."

"Coach Lawrence?"

"Yes, but I don't think he's in charge either. Maybe. I don't know. Vince and Billy Wilson are the ones who moved me."

"What about Jayden?" Maverick asked.

She shook her head. "I don't think he's involved. Jacob wasn't either, not really, but he knew too much. Heard Vince and Billy talking during a football practice." She swiped tears from her face. "Now, Jacob is dead."

"We'll find out who killed him. I promise." Blair laid a hand on her arm. "Anything else you can tell us before we take you back?"

"My father wants me to be a lure. I'm not sure if that's the right term, but he wants me to help coerce girls so Vince and Billy can take them. He said they'd trust me." She shuddered. "I won't do it. I won't."

"We can have you put into protective custody, Brittney." Blair stood.

"No, I can't have my father get too suspicious. As soon as he does, Lilly will be moved. Can I go back now?"

"Yes." Maverick took her by the elbow. "Be careful, Brittney. You've been a big help."

She cast wide eyes up at him. "Is my father going to jail?"

"For a very long time."

"Good." She marched toward his truck. "I'll be listening to everything real close and let y'all know everything I find out. My mom doesn't know a thing."

"Be careful." Blair fell into step beside her. "Doing that will be dangerous."

"My father might hit me, but he won't kill me."

No, but he might sell her far away. Maverick couldn't let that happen. He helped the girl into the truck, then drove a block away from the bank. "Play sick if you're caught. That would explain some time in the bathroom."

"I've got it. Thanks." She jumped out, slammed the door, and dashed down the alley.

"The cowed little girl is gone." He glanced at Blair.

"I think that went away when I told her Lilly was missing. We can't let anything happen to her, Maverick."

"We won't." He'd do everything in his power to

keep that promise. "Time to let the sheriff know. Once he does, Pitts will be locked up, right along with Vince and Billy."

She nodded. "Now, we need proof that Lawrence is involved."

He kept his gaze locked on hers. "I wish you weren't involved in this."

"It's my job."

"I know, but things are going to get real ugly. We're getting close, Blair. That means the person in charge will be getting desperate. Dangerous." He cupped her cheek. "I don't want anything to happen to you."

"It won't. We're being careful. I'm never alone. All we do is ask questions and relay what we find out to the sheriff's department."

"Someone is going to try and shut us up because you didn't heed the warnings."

She shrugged and leaned into his touch. "Let them try. I won't stop until they're stopped. The girls of Misty Hollow have been lucky so far. They might not have been if we weren't here working on their behalf. This town is counting on us."

He wrapped his hand around to the back of her head and pulled her close. "Then, let's not let them down." He kissed her.

Something popped.

The truck leaned to the side.

Another pop blew a hole in the windshield.

He shoved Blair down. "Someone is shooting at us."

Barely peering over the dashboard, he pressed the gas and rocketed the truck down the alleyway, praying whoever was shooting at them didn't know they'd spoken to Brittney just minutes before.

Chapter Sixteen

"We're going to crash!" Blair grabbed the overhead handle to her right. Another tire had been shot out, leaving them on two rims and two good tires. They weren't going to get out of this one.

"No, we're not." Maverick steered the truck to the side of the road and slammed on the brakes. "Get out and stay down. Head for the ditch, then call 911." He climbed into the passenger seat and followed her out.

Blair hunkered down in the ditch and dialed the sheriff's office. Diamond whined next to her.

After explaining their predicament, she found herself hauled to her feet and pulled under a barbed wire fence. Her shirt snagged, and she yanked free. "Where are we going?"

"The bar is about a mile across this field." He shot her a quick look. "Unless you want to go home?"

"No. Let's end this." Keeping her hand in his, she ran as fast as she could away from the sound of tires on gravel that alerted her to the fact that the shooter had pulled off the Interstate. No matter how fast they ran, she and Maverick couldn't outrun a bullet. They'd be exposed in the open pastureland.

"Stay close," he said.

"I'm not going anywhere you don't."

Her thighs burned, and her breath came in gasps by the time they climbed through another fence that bordered the property of the local bar. A sign that flashed multiple colors at night announced The Misty Bar. Simple.

With a sharp glance around, Maverick shoved open the door before pushing Blair into the dim recesses and ordering Diamond to stay. A long, polished, but nicked counter ran along one wall. Opposite that stood a plywood stage. Separating the two were multiple tables surrounding a dance floor.

"Y'all looking for someone?" The bartender, a burly, bald-headed man, stopped wiping a glass. "We don't open for another hour."

Blair glanced around. Two men huddled at a table in the corner. "Looks like you're doing business."

The bartender shrugged. "Some come in to conduct business meetings."

Right. Since one of the men was Coach Lawrence, she'd like to know what kind of meeting they conducted.

"Our business is with you." Maverick pulled out a bar stool for Blair before perching on one for himself. "I'm sure you're aware of the trouble we're having in Misty Hollow?"

"Yep. Sad." He set the glass aside and grabbed another one. "Not sure what I can help you with."

Blair jerked her head toward the two men in the corner. "Does the coach meet here often with people? Mr. Pitts in particular?"

"Ma'am, folks talk to me when they've been

drinking. It's my policy not to violate their privacy."

"Even if it impedes a murder investigation?" She arched a brow.

He frowned. "I haven't heard of a murder."

Since Maverick seemed content to let her take the lead, she answered, "A young high school boy was found dead in the lake."

"Suicide, I heard."

"We believe differently. Maverick here is deputized. We can get a warrant, question you at the station…"

"Fine, but I'm not sure how much help I can be." He glanced at the coach. "Yeah, him and Pitts come in here a lot. Never this early, though. I'd figure the coach should be at school."

So did she. At least he couldn't be the shooter. "Who's the man with him?"

"An outsider. Never seen him before."

"You've never spoken to him?"

"Nope. He came in, took a seat, then a few minutes later, Lawrence joined him. They've been there about fifteen minutes. I'll run them off soon if they don't order something." He narrowed his eyes. "You two look like you've been through some rough stuff."

"Truck broke down," Maverick interjected. "Mind if I use your phone? Mine is dead."

"Other end of the bar. No long distance."

Maverick slid from his stool and went to make a call or pretend to make one, Blair wasn't sure. Maybe he thought the bartender would be more talkative to a woman alone. She mentally shrugged.

"Any conversations raise any spider senses?"

He laughed. "This isn't the movies, lady."

Blair pressed her lips together and gave him the look her mother used to give her when she wasn't cooperating. "You know what I mean."

"Sure, I do, lady." He chuckled. "There is one thing…that man the coach is talking to isn't the only one he's met with besides Pitts. It's all been real secretive. My server said they stop talking when she serves them. She'll be here any minute. Maybe she can tell you something. Lawrence doesn't sit at the bar, so I'm not privy to his conversations."

"Do you get many secret conversations here?"

"It's a bar on a lonely highway. If folks want to talk unseen, this is the place to do it."

She supposed so. From the corner of her sight, she spotted Maverick ducking into the men's room. She swiveled on her stool. Coach Lawrence was no longer seated next to the stranger. Seeing her opportunity, Blair took the coach's empty seat.

"Welcome to Misty Hollow."

The man crossed his arms and sat back. "You're a pretty one, but you don't look the type to frequent bars before noon."

"I'm not the type to frequent them at any time." She smiled. "Just passing the time. I'm Blair Oakley, Search and Rescue."

"Right. The missing girls. Heard about them."

"What did you hear?"

"That you found them. You and that cowboy that followed Lawrence into the bathroom." His eyes hardened, his smile not reaching his eyes. "Good job."

"Thanks." She did her best to look nonchalant. "You didn't give me your name."

"Nope. No need. I'm just passing through."

"What's your business with the coach?"

"My business." He folded his hands on the tabletop. "Mind your own business or that pretty nose will get you in trouble."

"Is that a threat?"

"No, just passing along what I've seen happen. Oh, look. Your backup has arrived."

Blair turned to see Sheriff Westbrook darkening the door. He marched to their table.

"Howdy, Bill."

"Sheriff."

"Thought you'd be teaching science."

"Took a day off."

Another teacher?

~

Maverick turned from the sink as the coach exited one of the stalls. "Hey, Coach."

"Maverick." The man washed his hands.

"Day off?"

"Early release."

Very early release. "Truck broke down. Waiting on a ride."

"Bad luck." He pulled a handful of paper towels from the dispenser, dried his hands, and reached for the door.

"Kind of early to frequent the bar."

"Mind your own business. You and Miss Oakley don't know what you're interfering with." With a sharp look, he exited the room.

A threat was as good as an admission of guilt in Maverick's book. He grinned and returned to the front to see Blair and the sheriff with the stranger in time to hear the last of their conversation. Nothing too suspicious about one teacher meeting another, but the coach's warning in the men's room set off bells.

"Heard you broke down." The sheriff gave him a nod. "Your truck's been towed to the garage." He glanced at the other two men. "Be careful out there. We've got a shooter."

They exchanged a glance then nodded.

Maverick and Blair followed the sheriff from the bar. Outside, Maverick held the back door open for Blair and Diamond, then climbed into the front passenger seat. "Get any clues from my truck?"

"Only that you were shot at. Tire tracks behind your truck. Footprints following yours into the field." The sheriff turned the key in the ignition. "Other than that, we got nothing. You?"

"Coach Lawrence warned me and Blair to stop nosing around."

"I got the same warning from the other guy."

"Dunlap. Bill Dunlap teaches high school science." He gave a heavy exhale. "I'll have them brought in for questioning. Maybe it's time the two of you stepped back from this case. I don't want you killed."

"That makes three of us," Maverick said. "Problem is...we're in this up to our necks now. We might as well see it through."

"As long as you know the danger."

Maverick glanced back at Blair. "I think we do."

"Absolutely," she said. "And we're seeing this through."

The sheriff nodded. "When this is over, Miss Oakley, the sheriff's department could use someone like you on staff. Think about it."

"I will." Her eyes shimmered as her gaze met Maverick's.

His heart leaped. She might be sticking around. Something that made him very happy indeed. They hadn't had time to explore a possible relationship after the kiss on the mountain. He really would like to have the chance. Now, he might have one.

The sheriff drove them to the station to fill out an incident report, then offered them a ride to the garage. Maverick declined. They hadn't eaten in several hours and the diner was in walking distance from the sheriff's office and the garage walking distance from there.

"I don't like the two of you exposed like that." The sheriff frowned.

"If we hide, we'll never draw out who is responsible for what's going on." Blair hitched her chin. "We'll stay vigilant. This isn't the first time I've been threatened in my line of work."

It was the first time since Maverick became a victim, but he agreed with Blair. They couldn't go into hiding.

At the diner, they left Diamond outside where the dog curled up in the shade of a tree, before sitting at a booth where they could keep an eye on her. Maverick glanced at the daily special. BLT. No, thank you. His hunger was too big for a sandwich.

Blair's not so much. "Can I have cream cheese instead of mayo?"

The server smiled. "Absolutely. How crisp do you like your bacon?"

"Not charred."

"I'll have the chicken fried steak with extra gravy." Maverick handed over his menu. Once the server left, he directed his attention to Blair. "Nice offer the sheriff made you."

"Very, and unexpected."

"What do you think?" He held his breath.

Her cheeks turned rosy. "How wonderful it might be to take him up on the offer. Despite this case, I think I would like living in Misty Hollow. Maybe I'll start looking for a house to rent."

"Why not buy?"

"Renting is best." She took a deep breath. "In case things don't work out."

Meaning, in case she chose not to be with him. At least that's how he took her excuse. "Probably the best option."

"Yeah," she said softly.

When they caught those responsible for the abductions and the murder of Jacob, Maverick was going to kiss Blair senseless, then demand that she tell him where he stood with her. If she didn't want him, he'd walk away. No problem, but he needed to know. One way or the other. Then, if she still stayed, he'd avoid going to town as much as possible. Cowardly, yes, but he wouldn't be able to face her after making a fool of himself.

"What's wrong?" she asked softly.

"Nothing. Just thinking. What did Dunlap say to you?"

"That I'd lose my pretty nose if I didn't stop sticking it where it didn't belong. You?"

"Pretty much the same, except Lawrence didn't call me pretty." He grinned.

"Well, I don't think you're pretty either." Her eyes softened. "I think you're gorgeous and not just on the outside."

Be still his heart. If a bullet took him at that moment, he'd die a happy man. He wanted to tell her those exact words, but the arrival of the server stopped him. The diner wasn't the place to pour out his heart. God willing, he'd get his chance to say what needed to be said.

"What's the plan?"

Her question pulled him from his thoughts. "I don't have one."

"It's obvious, Dunlap and Lawrence are involved." She crossed her arms. "We need to prove it."

He sighed. They'd be painting bigger targets on their backs. "What are you thinking?"

"It's time to start accusing people outright. Make them mad. Angry people make mistakes."

Good Lord, she was going to get them killed.

Chapter Seventeen

Brittney pressed her ear to the door. Her suspicions rose, pulling her from bed in the middle of the night when she heard Vince Matterson's voice. Then her father's. Why would her father have business with a high school student at that time of the night?

"Things are getting very hot," her father said. "We've got to step things up."

"What do you want me to do?" Vince's voice wavered. "I have a future in football. I can't go to jail."

"You should've thought of that before getting involved. None of us are getting out of this now."

Brittney's heart lodged in her throat. If she'd had any doubts about her father's involvement before, she didn't now.

"I thought you were going to force Brittney to work for us." Vince's voice rose. "She'd be less suspicious."

"That was the plan, but she isn't cooperating. I haven't been stern enough with her."

Brittney gasped, clamping a hand over her mouth. She'd never work for them. Never!

"Did you hear something?" Vince asked. Footsteps approached the door.

Brittney fled down the hall to the kitchen. She had to get out of the house. If they found out she'd been eavesdropping...she didn't doubt her father would look the other way while she was killed or worse, sent away.

She snatched her mother's cell phone from the charger in the kitchen and slipped it into the backpack hanging on a hook. She'd already dropped her phone inside before heading for bed. Tomorrow was supposed to be the first day her father was allowing her to return to school. She supposed that wouldn't happen now.

She slipped out the back, holding the screen door so it didn't slam, then darted away from the house. Avoiding streetlights as much as possible, she kept to the shadows until she'd gone three blocks. Then, she pulled out her phone and dialed the number the nice cowboy had given her.

"This is Brittney Pitts. I need your help."

~

Maverick sat upright, blinking the sleep from his eyes. "Where are you?"

"Third Street behind the ice cream place. Hurry. It won't take long for them to know I'm gone."

"On my way." He grabbed the clothes he'd dropped on the floor before going to bed, then called Blair. "Brittney needs us."

"Ready in one minute."

Maverick dressed on his way out of his cabin. By the time he reached his truck, Blair and Diamond were sprinting across the yard. He started the engine as they climbed inside. "She's behind the ice cream parlor."

"It'll take us at least fifteen minutes to get there

and that's if you speed."

"Oh, I'll be flying, sweetheart." A young girl's life might depend on him.

"Not too fast. We can't help her if we're dead."

He cut her a sharp glance. "Okay, Miss Obvious."

"Sorry. I'm nervous about what happened to send her on the run."

"So, am I. She'll be okay." He reached for her hand, gave it a gentle squeeze, then returned his hand to the steering wheel. "Where can we take her? The ranch?"

"She'd be safe there, I think, but I'm going to call the sheriff." She punched his number into her phone. After explaining the situation, she turned her attention back to him. "He said he'll meet us at his office and will take over from there."

"Okay." He doubted his boss would've minded, but he preferred not springing an eyewitness in a possible trafficking case on him.

Once off the mountain, he drove the alleys until he pulled behind the ice cream parlor. Leaving the truck's lights on, he exited the vehicle and scanned the area for Brittney.

She emerged from behind a dumpster and darted toward him. Without a word, Blair held the door open for her, and the girl climbed in beside Diamond. "Hurry. I saw my father driving by about five minutes ago."

"He won't go where we're going." Maverick drove to the sheriff's office.

Sheriff Westbrook had the front door open when they pulled up. His sharp gaze scanned the road. "Inside before you're seen."

They raced for the door and inside where the sheriff led them to his office, informing the receptionist not to let anyone who asked know they were there. "I'm off for the night, and you haven't seen these folks."

"Got it."

In his office, he closed his door and shut the blinds. "You're safe here, Brittney. Can I get you something to eat or drink?"

The girl shook her head.

"Okay, sit down and tell me what is going on." He sat in his chair.

Maverick stood in front of the door to prevent anyone from entering. Diamond sat next to him, her ears alert while Blair took Brittney's hand and chose the chair next to her.

His blood boiled as he listened to Brittney recount the conversation between her father and Vince. He had no doubt in his mind now that the two were involved up to their hairline. What he didn't know was the identity of the one in charge.

"Anyone else been paying visits to your father?" the sheriff asked.

"Not that I know of." Brittney twisted the hem of her tee shirt. "But my father leaves the house a lot. He might tell my mother where he goes, but not me."

"He takes you to the bank with him?"

She nodded.

"Anyone visit him there?"

"Lots of people. It's his job." She wadded her tee shirt tighter. "There's a lock on the basement door. I think he's holding Lilly in there."

The sheriff met Maverick's gaze. "Okay, Brittney, you've been a big help. My wife is going to come and take you to our place. You'll be safe there, but we might need you to identify some people at some point. Can you do that?"

She jerked upright. "My father was going to use me to do bad things, Sheriff. I'll be happy to help."

~

Blair stood at the window as Brittney climbed into a jeep driven by the sheriff's wife. They lived somewhere on the other side of the mountain, from what she knew. Hopefully, Brittney would be safe there. It wasn't common for law enforcement to take witnesses to their home, was it?

"You okay?" Maverick stepped beside her.

"Yes, just hoping Brittney will be. She's been through a lot."

Two squad cars pulled in front of the building and four deputies, all wearing bullet proof vests, approached the building. They marched past Blair and Maverick and into the sheriff's office. A few minutes later, they marched back outside.

The sheriff stopped before following. "We're going to round up Pitts and the boy. You're welcome to stay, but out of sight. You can watch the proceedings from the other side of the interrogation mirror. Go there when you see us pull up."

Blair nodded. Things were almost over. Soon, she had a very big decision to make. Actually, she knew what she wanted. She glanced at Maverick. To stay in Misty Hollow.

For the next hour, she paced between the vending machine and the water fountain. Anxiety and anticipation coursed through her.

"Sit, Blair, before you wear a hole in the floor."

Maverick motioned to a chair next to her as headlights pierced the blinds.

"They're here." She rushed to the room the sheriff had told them to stay in.

A few minutes later, Mr. Pitts was led to the interrogation room. Two deputies escorted Billy and Vince down the hall, all wearing cuffs.

Pitts sat and glared across the table at the sheriff. "What is this outrage? How dare you stop me."

"What are you doing out past midnight with two underage teens, Mr. Pitts?" The sheriff sat after offering the man water or coffee which he declined.

"Taking them home. They'd been at the house too late visiting my daughter."

Sheriff Westbrook smiled. "Is that so?"

"Yep." The man crossed his arms. "Now tell me what this is about."

"It's about you being involved in the abduction of not only your daughter, but Lesley Bean and Lilly McClintock who is still missing. A warrant has been issued for a search of your house. What will we find there, Mr. Pitts?"

The man paled. "I have nothing to hide."

"I think differently." The sheriff folded his hands on the table and leaned closer. "I think you have a lot to hide. I believe we'll find evidence to that fact when we search your house. Deputies are headed there now. If we find out you're involved, you'll be going away for a very long time."

Pitts stiffened. "You won't find anything."

"For your sake, let's hope so. Will Billy and Vince have different stories?"

"I have no idea what those two do in their spare

time."

Blair shook her head. "The lies roll off him. Look at his eyes. He can't meet the sheriff's."

"Let's hope the deputies find Lilly."

"If Lilly McClintock is found in your basement, or evidence she was there, Mr. Pitts, we'll be bringing in your wife," the sheriff said.

"She's done nothing."

"For her sake, you might want to spare her the trauma of being hauled in wearing handcuffs." The sheriff's smile never faded.

Blair would've been intimidated sitting across from the man, and she didn't intimidate easily.

Pitts glanced at the mirror. "Whoever put you up to this will be sorry. It's my reputation at stake. I am not the one in control of these abductions."

"He didn't say he didn't know about them," Maverick said softly. "Only that he's not in charge."

"It's usually their own words that trip them up." She took a deep breath through her nose and released it slowly through her mouth. Some of the pent-up tension in her shoulders disappeared. They were close to ending this nightmare."

"We'll let you know what we find, Mr. Pitts." The sheriff stood.

"What are you doing with me now?"

"Holding you until my deputies return. Then, I'll let you know." The sheriff motioned to the door where a woman deputy entered and led Pitts away.

The interviews with Vince and Billy went better. Fear and worry radiated off the boys, especially Billy who was more than happy to spill his guts and gave the name of the man in charge. Science teacher Bill

Dunlap.

"I hate that we share the same first name," the boy sobbed.

"Then why did you do this?" the sheriff asked.

"Money. We got paid real good for luring in the girls."

"We?"

He nodded. "Me and Vince. Jacob knew about, but he refused." He swiped his arm across his nose and eyes.

"Who killed Jacob?"

"Mr. Dunlap. He said we couldn't leave any loose ends."

"You've been a big help, Billy."

"Can I go now?" Tears streamed down his face.

"Sorry, son, but the only place you're going is jail." The sheriff marched from the room.

"He said he'd kill us if we didn't do what he said!"

Blair tried to feel sorry for the young man and failed. He and Vince were old enough to know what they were doing. You didn't have to be a genius to know that kidnapping and selling young girls was wrong.

"Looks like this is almost over." Maverick gave a sad smile. "I hate to see these young people involved in something like this, but yet they were. Whatever future they had planned for themselves is gone now."

"They almost took the future away from those girls." Blair turned and left the room, running into Deputy Hudson. "What did you find?"

"Lilly McClintock, alive and well."

"And Dunlap?" Maverick asked.

"Gone. No sign of him. His car is missing from the garage, front door left unlocked. The man left in a hurry."

Pitts laughed from behind them as another deputy led him to a holding cell. "The two of you had better watch your backs. Dunlap isn't afraid to kill."

No, he wasn't, as evidenced by poor Jacob. Blair squared her shoulders. Let him come. Together, she and Maverick would meet him head on and come out victorious.

Chapter Eighteen

Blair, coffee cup in hand, stepped onto the back deck of the main house on The Rocking W as Diamond sniffed for a place to do her business. Occasionally, the dog would stop, point her ears toward the woods at the far end of the property, but would return to sniffing.

According to further questioning of Billy and Vince, they received confirmation that Dunlap led the trafficking group in Misty Hollow. No one seemed to know who gave him the orders. Pitts still refused to talk, saying to do so would endanger his family. Mrs. Pitts had been given the all clear of any wrongdoing. All she seemed guilty of was spending her days in a prescription drug induced haze.

Blair sighed. Maybe she would too if she were married to such a man as Pitts. With her father behind bars, Brittney had returned home. No one had seen any sign of Dunlap.

The crunch of gravel out front announced a visitor. Blair headed that way to see Maverick doing the same, donning a shirt as he did. His wet hair testified to the fact he'd gotten out of the shower.

"Just the two I want to see." Sheriff Westbrook

waited next to his car. "A couple of hunters saw a man matching Dunlap's description on the north side of the mountain. He had a backpack and a rifle. I'd like the two of you to see whether you can track him. From a distance. We'll be searching from the air. Do not approach the suspect. He's armed and dangerous. Here's a shirt he had hanging in his room. Hope it helps." He handed them a blue polo shirt before driving away.

Maverick glanced at Blair, his eyes dark, then nodded. "We can head right out."

"Thanks. Be prepared to spend some time out there. If you find a trail, I'd rather it not get cold."

"I'll pack some sleeping bags."

It wouldn't be the first time she'd spent the night alone in the woods with Maverick, but now, after the kiss they'd shared, doing so seemed a whole lot more intimate. "We'll find him, Sheriff."

"If anyone can, you and that wonderful dog can." He tipped his hat and got back in his car, rolling down the window. "Take a radio." He handed one out the window. "Keep an open line of communication at all times. Dunlap is a desperate man on the run."

After the sheriff left, Maverick headed for the house. "I'll have Mrs. White pack us some grub, then saddle the horses. They might give us some leverage over a man on foot."

Blair wasn't very comfortable on horseback, but he was right. They needed any advantage they could get. She headed to her room to pack a bag with a change of clothes. With no rain in the forecast, they should stay dry enough.

Half an hour later, she climbed into the saddle of a

roan mare, a bedroll tied behind her and gripped the reins.

"Loosen your hold." Maverick smiled. "Daisy will pretty much do things on her own."

"Okay." She did her best and hoped she didn't hurt the horse's mouth.

When Maverick urged his horse forward, hers followed. Easy.

Diamond loped alongside them.

After a few hours, they reached where Dunlap was last spotted and climbed from their horses. Blair gave Diamond the command to find and opened a water bottle while the dog searched for a scent.

When Diamond let out a bark and glanced her way, Blair sighed and returned to the saddle. "Go, girl."

The dog set off, Maverick and Blair on her tail. After swiping several low hanging branches away from her face, Blair figured walking might have been easier. She glared at Maverick's strong back. The man seemed unfazed, merely ducking under the branches. When one threatened to knock off his cowboy hat, he set it more firmly on his head and kept going.

The cowboy way or strictly Maverick? Either one, she could use a bit of his tolerance. Sweat poured down her face, and she glared at the sun. Pleasant days had turned to summer almost overnight.

Diamond lost the trail at the creek and darted back and forth before picking the scent back up on the other side. The horses splashed through the shallow water, wetting Blair's shoes.

Her backside felt raw and bruised. She wanted to call out for a break but didn't want to appear weak. Catching Dunlap meant they continued on. She couldn't be a baby. Not with so much at stake. So, she shoved aside her discomfort and focused on the man in front of her.

Maverick smiled over his shoulder, then sobered. "You okay?"

"Yes." Her discomfort must have showed on her face because he stopped and dismounted. "Ten-minute break."

"Diamond, stay." Blair slid from the saddle. Her legs buckled under her. Maverick rushed forward and grabbed her before she fell.

"I'm sorry. You aren't used to a long time in the saddle." He helped her to a pile of moss and dried leaves. "Sit. I'll get your water bottle."

"No more than ten minutes. We have to catch Dunlap." She wanted to lay back and stretch her aching body.

"We will."

She hoped so. The man wasn't a novice to the woods. His trail kept disappearing. Thankfully, Diamond was one of the best tracking dogs in the state and always picked his scent back up.

A twig snapped nearby. Blair jerked and glanced at Diamond. When the dog didn't appear alarmed, she relaxed and allowed herself the luxury of laying flat in the leaves.

~

Maverick felt like an uncaring scoundrel. He should know Blair couldn't sit for hours in the saddle. She wasn't a cowhand. Still, he couldn't stop glancing at his watch. They needed to catch Dunlap before nightfall. Once it grew dark, it became almost impossible to see in the woods, and he didn't relish spending the night in the shadows with an unscrupulous man who would do anything to escape being caught.

Even kill.

His gaze landed on the dozing Blair. He couldn't let her be harmed. Dunlap wasn't the only one who would do anything to get what he wanted. Maverick would too if it meant keeping Blair safe.

With a sigh, he nudged her awake. "I'm sorry, but we need to get moving."

"I know." She groaned and got to her feet. "I'll rest when this is all over."

"If we don't find him soon, we'll be spending the night out here."

"At least it isn't raining." She groaned again as he helped her into the saddle. "I'm not going to ride a horse again for a long time."

He chuckled. "The more you ride, the easier it gets."

"Well, I'm not going to find out anytime soon. Search, Diamond."

Nose to the ground, the dog set off and led them higher up the mountain. A helicopter circled overhead. Seeing anything from the sky through the dense foliage would be almost impossible until they reached the top where the trees would thin. Even then, he didn't think Dunlap dumb enough to stay in the open for long.

His phone dinged. A glance at the screen showed a text from the sheriff. A woman had come forth stating that Dunlap had been with her each of the times that a girl had gone missing. Maverick texted back asking whether they should call off the search and head back. The sheriff replied no because Dunlap was still a suspect and his running off suspicious. Maverick related the texts to Blair.

"He could've paid the woman to lie for him," she said. "It happens all the time."

"If that's the case, I'm sure the sheriff will find out." Maverick slid his phone back into his pocket. A solid alibi for Dunlap could make their search fruitless, but he'd continue until the sheriff said to stop.

By nightfall, Blair looked ready to fall out of her saddle. Maverick called a halt in a small clearing next to a creek and tethered the horses near a small patch of grass after helping an exhausted Blair from the saddle.

"I'll spread out the sleeping bags and dig through our packs for something for supper." She untied the roll behind her saddle.

"Mrs. White packed sandwiches, I think. We don't want to risk a fire and give ourselves away if Dunlap is close." He removed the saddles from the horses and gave them a quick brush down.

After taking care of the horses, he joined Blair and sat on his sleeping bag. "The ground won't be the most comfortable bed."

"I've slept on worse than a bed of leaves." She smiled and handed him a sandwich. "Things could be worse. It could be raining, we could have teenagers playing an eerie recording, or a madman holding us at gunpoint."

"Let's hope none of that happens." He grinned and bit into a thick ham and cheese sandwich before accepting a cup of lukewarm coffee from Blair. "We'll get him tomorrow."

"I hope so." Weariness lined her face. "Once, I searched for three days before finding a missing child. Thankfully, the boy was found alive, but cold and hungry. This is the first time I've been part of a search for a potential killer."

"Let's hope it's the last time." They had the statement of both Billy and Vince saying Dunlap killed Jacob. The man wasn't a potential killer, but a cold-blooded one.

He finished the sandwich and cold coffee, then checked his weapon. He'd sleep with it close at hand that night.

"I hope we don't need that," Blair said softly.

"Are you armed?" He glanced up.

"I've got one in my pack."

He started to tell her to keep it close but held his tongue. If Dunlap got the drop on them, he'd take Maverick's gun. If he didn't know about Blair's, they might turn things in their favor.

He scoffed at his optimism. Things didn't usually go the way he planned. They hadn't in the Middle East or the fire where he'd received his burns. What made him think things would be different this time?

She did. Blair might be exhausted, but she'd not once said they wouldn't find Dunlap or that things would go wrong. He needed to adopt her attitude and believe things would work out. Her optimism and perseverance were two of the reasons he loved her.

Loved. He never thought he'd say those words about any woman.

He rubbed his jaw through his beard. His scars didn't bother her. She'd seen him without his shirt, touched him, kissed him. Blair Oakley was a remarkable woman. A woman he wanted to pursue a relationship with, maybe spend the rest of his life with. When this was over.

"What are you thinking?" she asked softly.

"About what I'm going to do when this is over."

"What's that?"

"Wait for your answer regarding the sheriff's offer."

She ducked her head.

"Have you decided?" His heart stilled.

"Almost."

"Well, we're all in a dither about the answer to that question." Dunlap, gun in hand, stepped from the trees. When Diamond made a move toward him, he swung the gun in her direction. "Call her off, Miss Oakley, or you won't have a dog."

"Diamond, go."

The dog whined, cast a glance in Blair's direction, then raced into the trees.

Dunlap smiled. "Smart animal." The gun returned to Blair. "Your weapon, Maverick. Toss it toward me or I'll shoot her."

Maverick pulled his weapon and tossed it aside. "Now what?"

"Figured you were up here looking for me, so here I am."

"Again, now what?"

"That's up to the two of you. On your feet."

Chapter Nineteen

Blair eyed the pack behind her horse's saddle. She'd never reach her gun before being shot herself. Pushing to her feet, she glanced at Maverick who stood, hands out.

"Now, set the horses free." Dunlap motioned in their direction. "I'm sure they know their way home, and we'll be long gone before they alert the other cowboys that something is amiss."

Maverick moved at a snail's pace. Blair kept her attention on the man with the gun until they were ordered to move.

"The two of you should've minded your own business," Dunlap muttered. "This is all on you."

Blair's heart lodged in her throat. Her blood chilled at his ominous tone. What did he have planned for them? It wouldn't be good.

"In front of me, side-by-side, where I can see you," Dunlap ordered. "Don't worry. We won't be together for long."

Blair stepped close enough to Maverick for their shoulders to touch, drawing strength from him. He took her hand in his and whispered that things would be okay.

Would they? They had no weapon and no horses. Not even Diamond, thankfully. The dog would put herself in harm's way in order to protect Blair. Still, she missed her four-legged friend's company who she was rarely without. At least she had Maverick for whatever waited for them.

Dunlap kept them moving through the increasing night. No one spoke. Since Blair didn't know the mountain, she prayed Maverick had a plan for their escape.

"Through that crevice in the rock." Dunlap had them turn left. "We're headed to your final resting place."

Maverick's hold on Blair's hand tightened. "It'll be okay."

"It won't. He's going to kill us."

"Whispers carry far in the night." Dunlap chuckled behind them. "Yes, I plan on killing you. The two of you won't see sunrise, but hey. At least you'll be together."

She'd never have the chance to tell Maverick how she felt about him. That she couldn't imagine leaving Misty Hollow as long as he resided there. They would never know what the future held for them outside of the next few hours. Did they have a few hours or only minutes?

Should they try to run? She glanced over her shoulder. No, they couldn't outrun a bullet, but one of them might make it out alive. She'd rather that person be Maverick. He'd already lived through so much tragedy.

Yes. She'd distract Dunlap the best she could at

some point in order for Maverick to escape. She'd tell him to run for help, even knowing he'd never make it back in time to save her. Would he go if she asked him? Somehow, she'd make him go.

When they moved through the crevice between two boulders, a small hunting cabin came into view. The place didn't look as rundown as some she'd seen during their searches.

Inside, a cozy living space filled the one-room complete with a sofa, chair, small dinette set for four, and a galley style kitchen. A closed door suggested a bathroom, but without looking she couldn't tell for sure. It could be a closet.

"Each of you in one of the chairs, back-to-back. Put your hands behind you and hook your feet around the chair legs. Now." Dunlap waved the gun.

Exhaling heavily, Maverick released Blair's hand and turned the chairs to face away from each other before taking a seat. As Blair started to sit, he lunged to his feet, whipping a gun from the waistband of his pants.

"Well," Dunlap grinned. "You must've had that stashed on one of the horses." He aimed the gun at Blair. "Her or you. It doesn't matter to me."

The two men stared at each other for several tense minutes, before Dunlap started to count. When he started to say three, Maverick tossed the weapon onto the sofa.

Dunlap fired.

Maverick spun and hit the wall before sliding to the rough wooden floor.

Blair screamed. "You said you wouldn't shoot if he dropped the gun."

"I did not say that." Dunlap set his gun on the table and pulled zip ties from his back pocket. He secured her hands behind her, then each of her ankles to the chair legs. "I could leave the two of you to die of thirst and starvation, but those ranch hands would be here before then. I'm sure that dog of yours could track us easily enough."

She hissed as the tie cut into the flesh of her wrists. "Why are you doing this?"

"Because you're in the way."

"No, I mean the girls."

"Money. There's a lot of money in selling pretty little things." He stepped back, his eyes hard. "I contemplated selling you rather than killing you, but I think you'd be too much trouble in the end."

"I'm not in the right age bracket." She twisted her hands, biting her lip as the ties cut deeper.

"There are still buyers of lovely women your age." He stepped back, his gaze raking over her. "Pity that you'll be dead by morning. Yes, the younger girls fetch more, but you'd still bring in a pretty penny."

She glared up at him. "You're right. I'd be too much trouble."

He laughed and pulled up a chair to face her before sitting. "This is only a minor setback, Miss Oakley. I'll move on and start again. Or I could retire, I suppose. I've managed to put away a lot of money. Enough to live comfortably in a different country."

"Would you please check on Maverick?" Tears burned her eyes.

"Sure, but it won't matter whether he's dead or alive." He moved and checked for a pulse. "He's alive. At least you'll have his company as you draw your final breath." He gave her another once over, said again what a pity it was, then pulled a gas can from under the kitchen sink.

Fire? She watched in horror as he splashed the accelerant over the walls and front door. Then, he stepped outside, tossing the can aside and pulled a box of matches from his front pocket. "Adios, Miss Oakley." He struck the match and dropped it, igniting the gas. Tossing a little wave in her direction, he jumped from the porch.

Fierce barking reached Blair's ears. The man outside yelped, then gave a bloodcurdling scream.

Blair glanced at the gun on the table, then at the one on the sofa. Both were too far to do her any good. She struggled against her ties to no avail. "Diamond! Down girl." Her dog wasn't trained to kill, but from the screams coming from outside, she was doing a good job of causing damage. "Diamond. Here, girl!"

The flames continued to spread.

Diamond appeared in the doorway, then backed up and whined as the fire blocked her way.

"Get help, girl." She repeated the command when the dog whined. "Go."

With a sorrowful, brown-eyed gaze, the dog turned and left.

Dunlap cried for help outside showing her he still lived. She didn't know whether to be happy or upset that he still drew breath.

"Come untie me, and I'll help you!"

"I can't. Your dog tore up my leg."

Good. Blair bounced the chair closer to the wall, then threw herself backward. The impact knocked the breath from her body. Regaining control of her breathing, she repeated the process until the chair splintered under her.

Maverick groaned, spurring her into action.

She maneuvered herself until she had her hands down and under her legs until they were in front of her. Blood from where the plastic bit into her skin made work slippery. "Wake up, Maverick." She coughed as the room filled with smoke that circled around her and billowed out the door.

It would take Diamond hours to reach the ranch. It was up to Blair to get her and Maverick out of the building.

She brought her wrists to her mouth and tried biting through the plastic. She had to stop every few seconds to cough despite being on the floor and the smoke over her head. She rolled closer to Maverick. "Wake up, Maverick. I need you." A violent fit of coughing overtook her, halting her progress.

"Dunlap, you still out there?"

No answer. The man was either gone or unconscious. Blair had never felt more alone in her life.

"Not that he would help us," she mumbled, then returned to trying to chew her way free.

Smoke made her eyes water. Visibility lessened. Heat from the encroaching flames grew too warm for comfort. They were going to die.

She stopped struggling. Her wrists bled, her back ached from slamming against the wall, and her right ankle throbbed. For several minutes she gave into despair and pity before returning to what seemed like a futile effort to free herself.

The crackling of the flames blocked out any sound. Sobs shook her body. Tears and saliva slickened the plastic between her teeth until, there, her hands were free. Getting the binds off her ankles would require a different technique. She couldn't fold herself in half enough to chew on them.

Her gaze landed on the still form of Maverick. "I love you. I had planned on staying in Misty Hollow, taking the sheriff up on his offer. I'm sorry that won't happen now." Her sobs increased. "I'm sorry I've failed you. I can't get free…" Unless.

She pressed her back against the wall and pushed to her feet. There had to be something in the kitchen. A knife, scissors, anything. She couldn't shoot the tight binding from her ankle without shooting herself.

Wanting to see for herself how badly Maverick was injured, she bent over him and pressed her fingers to his neck. A weak but steady pulse greeted her touch. He lived, but the pool of blood spreading under him told her he didn't have much time. Freeing her feet would have to wait.

She shrugged out of her tee shirt. The sports bra she wore would be enough coverage. Now was not the time for modesty. She tied the shirt around the gunshot wound under his collar bone the best she could, taking comfort from the moan that escaped him. If he felt pain, then he lived. Finished, she turned her attention to a search for a knife.

The third kitchen drawer revealed a homemade butcher knife, it's blade dull. She sat on the floor, legs stretched out in front of her. Wood splints from the chair legs slowed her process as she started to saw.

"Hold on, Maverick. I'm going to get us out of here." She blinked away the smoke-caused tears and stifled a cough.

She hissed when the knife slipped and slicked her skin. Feeling pain worked for her and Maverick. She, too, still lived.

The flames had reached the roof letting her know she didn't have much time. She sawed harder. Finally, the plastic tie fell from one ankle to the other. Lunging to her feet, she gathered both guns, shoving them into her waistband, then grabbed Maverick's feet.

She struggled to pull him from the house, one tiny bit at a time until they reached the fresh air of the outdoors. She thumped him down the steps, apologizing for each bang of his head and shoulders until she had him a safe distance from the cabin.

She collapsed next to him, her breath coming in painful gasps.

The cabin gave a mighty groan as the ceiling fell.

She glanced around for sight of Dunlap. The man was nowhere to be seen. Spots of blood led into the trees on the north side of the clearing. He couldn't get far.

Diamond bounded to Blair's side.

"Naughty dog. I told you to go." Blair wrapped her arms around the dog's neck. Then, exhaustion won, and she lay next to Maverick.

Her eyes drifted closed.

Chapter Twenty

When Blair woke, Maverick still lay unconscious. She checked his vitals and makeshift bandage, relieved to see the bleeding had slowed. The bullet hadn't hit anything vital, thank God.

Getting to her feet, she lay one of the guns next to him, then took the other one and Diamond into the trees in search of Dunlap. Despite the fact she wouldn't mind him dead, she couldn't leave him lying somewhere wounded. She wasn't the animal he was.

The light of a full moon allowed her to see well enough as she searched the woods. Help should be coming soon. She estimated she'd slept maybe half an hour, but then again, Diamond hadn't gone for help as ordered. Help would depend on the two horses heading straight home. Until then, it was up to Blair to take care of things. This she could do much better than fighting a fire.

Her heart ached at how close she had come to giving up. If she had, both she and Maverick would be lying under a pile of smoldering rubble.

Grumbling from in front of her led her to where Dunlap sat against the trunk of a tree, his shirt tied tight around his thigh. He glared when she approached, then shrank back at the sight of Diamond. "Get that beast away from me. She tried to kill me."

"She isn't an attack dog."

"Could've fooled me."

"You were a threat to me." She knelt next to him. "Let me see your leg."

He eyed the gun in her hand.

"Don't try or I will sic my dog on you again."

He crossed his arms. "Fine."

She untied the shirt and grimaced. Puncture marks marred a now swollen thigh. Blood oozed from the bites. "You'll live, but this is on its way to getting infected."

"Why do you care? Leave me here to die."

"As despicable a man you might be, you are a human being. It goes against what I believe in to leave you out here as coyote food." She stood and propped a shoulder under his arm. "We'll head back to where I left Maverick and wait for the police."

"The cowboy's dead?" He smirked.

"Nope." She had to bite her tongue to keep from saying she wished Dunlap was. "I'd steer clear of him if I were you. He's going to be mad when he wakes up. How did you get into trafficking?"

"Stumbled into it. I was going to be a bookie for the horse races, but someone told me how easy it was to snatch and sell people."

"So, you recruited your students."

He shrugged. "They needed money for college. Guess that's off the table now."

"Pretty sure." She wanted to toss his arm from her shoulders and leave him to rot. "It didn't bother you at all?"

"Why would it? Everyone is out to make a buck somehow. That happens to be the career path I chose. On the side, of course."

"Of course." Her stomach rolled. The sooner she got this man to where Maverick was and the authorities arrived to take him off their hands the better.

~

"Blair!" Maverick bolted upright.

His gaze landed on the smoking pile that had once been a hunting cabin. They'd been in there. Dunlap had set the place on fire.

He turned and vomited, his body shuddering. "Blair!" He struggled to his feet, grimacing against the pain in his chest.

The tee shirt tied around his wound let him know she'd made it out of the building and pulled him to safety. Where was she? Where was the dog?

"I'm here." She emerged from the trees with Dunlap leaning on her and limping. She dumped him in the clearing and rushed to Maverick's side. "You're awake."

"I'll live." He cupped her face. "You saved us both. And him, it seems." He shot the man a glare he wished would've seared him to ashes. "What happened to him?"

"Diamond. She didn't leave us like I told her to."

"Good girl." He lowered back to the ground. "Did you find his pack? There might be something in there we can use. Water, a radio..." All of which he'd left in the pack on his horse.

"I didn't see one, but I'll check. Stay here. Don't kill him. You aren't that person." She dashed back into the trees.

"Looks like the woman is stronger than both of us." Dunlap sneered.

"I would've left you to rot in the woods."

The man laughed. "I did leave the two of you."

"You'll rot in prison."

"Maybe. But I have powerful friends on the outside. I might walk away from all this."

"Not on that leg." Maverick grinned. "Watch him, Diamond." He derived a great deal of pleasure at the way Dunlap recoiled from the dog who planted herself two feet away from him.

"Found it." Blair returned, holding a pack. "Granola bars, water, and a cell phone, but there's no service." She handed him something to eat and drink before tossing a water bottle toward Dunlap. At Maverick's frown, she added, "He's a person."

"Hmm. He barely fits that description." He drank half the bottle, washing the smoke from his throat, then handed the bottle back to her. "Are you injured in any way?"

"Just my wrists and ankles where the zip ties were." She held out her hands.

He wanted to throttle Dunlap at the sight of the raw, welts. They were no longer bleeding but looked painful.

Exhaustion ripped through him, the adrenaline fading now that she was safely back at his side. "We'll get you treated once help arrives."

"Not until that gunshot is looked at." She sat back on her haunches. "The bullet didn't exit, Maverick. I think that's why the bleeding has slowed, at least that we can see. You could be bleeding internally." Tears shimmered in her eyes. "You'll need surgery. I want you to stay still. I can handle things."

"Sweetheart, you've proven that you can." She'd been as strong as any of his military buddies, but once this was over, she'd collapse. He'd seen it before. Then, it would be his turn to help her through whatever nightmares might plague her when she closed her eyes. "Come here." He held out his good arm.

She snuggled against him, resting her head on his chest. "I thought I'd lose you, Maverick."

"I love you, too."

She jerked her gaze to his. "What?"

"I heard you when you said you loved me, that you were going to stay." He gave her a tender kiss. "I love you, too. I hope you weren't just saying that because you thought we were going to die."

"I didn't," she answered softly. "I meant every word. I was going to tell you again when this was all over."

"That would be nice." He smiled and kissed her again.

"There he goes." She waved to where Dunlap limp/ran away from them.

Maverick lifted the gun from the ground next to him and fired. The bullet kicked up dirt at the man's feet. "Get back here or we order the dog to attack."

The man cursed and made his way back.

"I wish I had something to tie him up with." Blair stood. "Your belt." She wiggled her fingers. "I can use yours on his feet and his on his hands."

"Make sure his hands are secured behind him." He shifted and removed his belt.

She bound his hands and feet before returning to

Maverick. "I need a nap."

Her face had paled, sending his heart dropping. He'd really hoped her strength would last until help arrived. "Go ahead. I'll keep an eye on him."

"There isn't much you can do as injured as you are."

"Diamond is here to help. Will she listen to me?"

"Yes." She curled up next to him and closed her eyes.

Maverick smoothed her hair from her face. They both smelled strongly of smoke and sweat but were alive. He sighed and glanced over to where Dunlap, too, had closed his eyes.

Soon, the welcome sound of horses and men's voices broke through the silence as the sun peered over the mountaintop. Help had finally arrived.

"Maverick." The sheriff shot a look at Dunlap, ordered a deputy to put the man on the back of a horse, then hurried to Maverick's side. "How badly are you injured?"

"Gunshot. Smoke inhalation. Blair has abrasions around her wrists and ankles. She got us out of that burning building, Sheriff. She'll make a good addition to your team."

He smiled. "Good to hear. Can you ride?"

"I'll do whatever I need to do to get out of here." He shook Blair awake, then stood. His legs trembled beneath him. "We're going home, sweetheart."

"Hey, sheriff. I'm accepting the job." She thrust out her hand.

He eyed the bloody grimy palm, then chuckled and returned the gesture. "So, I've heard. Let's get you two to the house. We'll have a chopper land in a field not far from here. Can you make it?"

"Absolutely. Dunlap shot Maverick and set the house on fire after tying us up inside. Diamond mangled his leg good, but I've bandaged it. Hope he rots in prison."

Maverick met the sheriff's amused gaze. "She's feisty."

"Appears that way. The two of you won't have to deal with Dunlap again until his trial. Let's get you to the hospital."

Blair called Diamond to follow, then climbed onto a horse behind Maverick. Her arms wrapping around his waist felt better than anything had in a very long time. The weight of her head on his back gave him hope for the future. Maverick had found the other half of himself in Blair Oakley. The missing half.

A helicopter waited a short ride away. Soon, they lifted into the air and zoomed toward the hospital in Langley. Once there, Maverick reluctantly relinquished Blair to the medics while he was wheeled away for surgery.

When he woke, the first thing he saw was Blair dozing in a chair beside his bed. "Why aren't you in a bed?"

~

Blair's eyes popped open. "I didn't want to leave you."

"How bad is the damage?"

"Not bad. No vital organs were hit. We were lucky, Maverick." She took his hand in hers.

"Because of you. If not for you, we'd both have burned in that building."

She smiled. "I couldn't let that happen. I know

how you feel about fires."

"Definitely not the way I want to leave this world."

She lifted his hand to her lips. "I hope that doesn't happen for a very long time."

When the doctor entered the room, she excused herself and headed for the closest restroom. Inside, she locked the door, then planted her hands flat on the sink to steady herself as she gave into the tears she'd been holding at bay.

The fear from the night before escaped with the tears, leaving her tired, but refreshed. The doctor who had tended to her wrists and ankles mentioned that shock would set in once the danger of death had gone.

Seeing Maverick lying in the hospital bed, pale and vulnerable, had almost been her undoing. When he'd opened his eyes, relief so palpable she could taste it had left her weak. Once she returned to the ranch, she'd sleep for days.

Taking a deep breath, she met her gaze in the mirror. The sheriff had called her a hero. She didn't agree. She'd simply been a woman intent on saving the life of the man she loved. As horrible as the night had been, she'd do it again if it meant Maverick's life.

After regaining self-control, she returned to his hospital room.

"The doc said I can get out of here tomorrow." He held out his hand and beckoned her forward. "Go home. Get some rest."

She shook her head. "There's something else I want to do."

"Which is?" He arched a brow.

"I found a house on five acres of land for sale. I'd

like to take a look at it, maybe put in an offer." She smiled. "Buy some chickens. The house is right outside of town."

"Not on the mountain?" He chuckled.

"Heavens, no. It's a beautiful mountain, but there are too many bad memories for me to live up there."

"Where does that leave me?" Hope shined in his eyes.

"I'm thinking I might need a search and rescue partner." She smiled. "We make a good team, don't you think?"

"Yes, ma'am, we do. Chickens sound nice. Maybe a horse or two." He waved his hand again, until she placed hers in his. "I know this is…sudden, but…marry me, Blair. As soon as I'm out of here. We can have a wedding later, if that's what you want, but I don't want to spend any more time away from you than I have to."

She grinned and glanced around the hospital room. "Not exactly the place I envisioned a wedding proposal when I was a little girl."

"Then, I'll wait until I'm out of here and do it proper."

"No, this is perfect. Yes, Maverick Browning, I will marry you. I don't need a fancy wedding."

"How does the Caribbean sound for a honeymoon? I'm sure the sheriff doesn't expect you to start work right away."

"I've always wanted to go there." She placed her cheek against the back of his hand. "Get well fast, Maverick. I'm not a patient woman."

He laughed. "Kiss me until I can't breathe and the monitor starts beeping."

"Naughty." She leaned over him and obliged.

The End

Dear Reader,

I hope you've enjoyed the adventure with Blair and Maverick as much as I have. Not all stories have a happy ending in real life, but here are those out there seeking justice.

Trafficking is a horrible reality that stalks the world. If you or anyone you know is a victim, **Get Help** 24/7 **1-888-373-7888**

There are people waiting to help.

God Bless,

Cynthia

www.cynthiahickey.com

Cynthia Hickey is a multi-published and best-selling author of cozy mysteries and romantic suspense. She has taught writing at many conferences and small writing retreats. She and her husband run the publishing press, Winged Publications. They live in Arizona and Arkansas, becoming snowbirds with three dogs. They have ten grandchildren who keep them busy and tell everyone they know that "Nana is a writer."

Connect with me on FaceBook
Twitter
Sign up for my newsletter and receive a free short story
www.cynthiahickey.com

Follow me on Amazon
And Bookbub
Shop my bookstore on shopify. For better prices and autographed books.

Enjoy other books by Cynthia Hickey

Cowboys of Misty Hollow
Cowboy Jeopardy

Misty Hollow
Secrets of Misty Hollow
Deceptive Peace

Calm Surface
Lightning Never Strikes Twice
Lethal Inheritance
Bitter Isolation
Say I Don't
Christmas Stalker
Bridge to Safety
When Night Falls
A Place to Hide
Mountain Refuge

Stay in Misty Hollow for a while. Get the entire series here!

The Seven Deadly Sins series
Deadly Pride
Deadly Covet
Deadly Lust
Deadly Glutton
Deadly Envy
Deadly Sloth
Deadly Anger

The Tail Waggin' Mysteries
Cat-Eyed Witness
The Dog Who Found a Body
Troublesome Twosome
Four-Legged Suspect
Unwanted Christmas Guest
Wedding Day Cat Burglar

Brothers Steele

Sharp as Steele
Carved in Steele
Forged in Steele
Brothers Steele (All three in one)

The Brothers of Copper Pass
Wyatt's Warrant
Dirk's Defense
Stetson's Secret
Houston's Hope
Dallas's Dare
Seth's Sacrifice
Malcolm's Misunderstanding
The Brothers of Copper Pass Boxed Set

Time Travel
The Portal

Tiny House Mysteries
No Small Caper
Caper Goes Missing
Caper Finds a Clue
Caper's Dark Adventure
A Strange Game for Caper
Caper Steals Christmas
Caper Finds a Treasure
Tiny House Mysteries boxed set

Wife for Hire – Private Investigators
Saving Sarah
Lesson for Lacey

Mission for Meghan
Long Way for Lainie
Aimed at Amy
Wife for Hire (all five in one)

A Hollywood Murder
Killer Pose, book 1
Killer Snapshot, book 2
Shoot to Kill, book 3
Kodak Kill Shot, book 4
To Snap a Killer
Hollywood Murder Mysteries

Shady Acres Mysteries
Beware the Orchids, book 1
Path to Nowhere
Poison Foliage
Poinsettia Madness
Deadly Greenhouse Gases
Vine Entrapment
Shady Acres Boxed Set

CLEAN BUT GRITTY Romantic Suspense

Highland Springs

Murder Live
Say Bye to Mommy
To Breathe Again
Highland Springs Murders (all 3 in one)

Colors of Evil Series

CYNTHIA HICKEY

Shades of Crimson
Coral Shadows

The Pretty Must Die Series

Ripped in Red, book 1
Pierced in Pink, book 2
Wounded in White, book 3
Worthy, The Complete Story

Lisa Paxton Mystery Series

Eenie Meenie Miny Mo
Jack Be Nimble
Hickory Dickory Dock
Boxed Set

Hearts of Courage
A Heart of Valor
The Game
Suspicious Minds
After the Storm
Local Betrayal
Hearts of Courage Boxed Set

Overcoming Evil series
Mistaken Assassin
Captured Innocence
Mountain of Fear
Exposure at Sea
A Secret to Die for

Collision Course
Romantic Suspense of 5 books in 1

INSPIRATIONAL

Nosy Neighbor Series
Anything For A Mystery, Book 1
A Killer Plot, Book 2
Skin Care Can Be Murder, Book 3
Death By Baking, Book 4
Jogging Is Bad For Your Health, Book 5
Poison Bubbles, Book 6
A Good Party Can Kill You, Book 7
Nosy Neighbor collection

Christmas with Stormi Nelson

The Summer Meadows Series
Fudge-Laced Felonies, Book 1
Candy-Coated Secrets, Book 2
Chocolate-Covered Crime, Book 3
Maui Macadamia Madness, Book 4
All four novels in one collection

The River Valley Mystery Series
Deadly Neighbors, Book 1
Advance Notice, Book 2
The Librarian's Last Chapter, Book 3
All three novels in one collection

Made in the USA
Monee, IL
09 June 2024